Unmasking Lady Helen

THE KINSEY FAMILY BOOK ONE

By

MAGGI ANDERSEN

Hear my soul speak:
The very instant that I saw you, did
My heart fly to your service.

The Tempest

Shakespeare

CHAPTER ONE

Queen's Walk, Green Park, London, 1821

"He's down there again."

"Come away from the window, Diana. He might see you." Helen eyed her sister as she arranged the cups and saucers over the table. "The sun's shining directly on your hair. You'll attract inappropriate attention."

"I will, in a minute."

Unable to resist a peek, Helen rose and joined Diana at the window. Down below, in the line of trees rimming the park, a man stood half in shadow. He stepped forward, and sunlight fell on his face. A chiaroscuro of light and shade delineated strong cheekbones, a chiseled chin, and a determined set to his shoulders before the shadows claimed him again.

Helen turned away, unwilling to give such a masculine figure another thought. "The tea will get cold."

"I can't see him. He must have gone." Diana let the lace curtain fall back into place and joined her at the table. "Another man has just walked away down the path."

"Were they together?"

"No, I don't think so."

Helen finished buttering each scone and added strawberry preserve. She found small domestic tasks soothing, although Diana had accused her of using them to hide from the world. "Did you send the footman yesterday to inquire if the man needed assistance?"

"I did, but he'd vanished into the park before Jeremy reached the bottom of the garden."

"Odd how he stands there alone for half an hour or more, a few yards from our back gate. He must be waiting for someone."

Diana sat beside her on the threadbare crimson plush sofa. She took the thick white ceramic cup and saucer that was part of the schoolroom china and stirred in sugar. "If it was someone from Kinsey House, he would have inquired at the door." She added a scone to her plate.

"If he comes again tomorrow, tell a servant to invite him down to the kitchen," Helen said. "Some have fallen on hard times since the war. We mustn't forget Father's wish to care for the less fortunate."

Diana chuckled. "He didn't look hungry, not in fashionable clothes and Hessians, and he carried a brass-topped cane."

"Then his business does not concern us." Helen arranged the small triangles of sandwiches neatly on a plate.

Diana dabbed her mouth with her napkin. "He's quite handsome."

"Can you discern that from the schoolroom window? We are three flights above ground." She'd thought the same. The cake knife poised to slice seed cake, she quickly dismissed an annoying flush of interest. It was merely him standing so still and intent when most strolled leisurely past along the Walk.

Helen offered Diana the plate, aware that her impulsive sister was about to indulge in one of her flights of fancy, some of which had led her into some awful scrapes in the past. "Your imagination is taking hold again. Next, you'll be saying there are ghosts living in the attic."

"Ghosts don't live, silly. They metamorphose and float around." Diana sipped her tea. "Perhaps I couldn't see his face so well, but he is tall and broad-shouldered. At one point, he took off his hat and ran his fingers through his wavy dark hair." She grinned. "It's the reason I first noticed him."

Helen smiled. "Perhaps he's one of Papa's classical scholars from Cambridge, composing a sonnet on wood nymphs. They're a peculiar lot if you ask me."

"But they all look pale and weedy, and he's not at all—"

"Papa isn't pale and weedy," Helen interjected.

"But Papa is always away riding camels and visiting hot climes." Diana gazed into space. "Perhaps this man is involved in a romantic liaison. And the lady has not kept her promise. She might have broken his heart."

Helen shook her head and laughed. She envied her sister's romantic view of the world. Helen's view was more than a little suspicious. Men who did not behave as one might expect were deserving of suspicion.

Their lanky younger brother entered the doorway and crossed the worn patterned carpet stalked by a black cat. "Who's broken whose heart?"

Diana shrugged. "It's of no importance. Purely a hypothetical supposition."

Helen dashed milk into a saucer and placed it on the floor. "Here, Plato."

The cat graciously accepted the offering and lapped the milk with its pink tongue.

Toby perched on the old rocking horse. Gripping its moth-eaten mane, he rocked gently, his knees almost under his chin. "Ham sandwiches, cake, and scones? Good, I'm starving. Pour me some tea, would you, Helen?"

"Toby, would you like to play shuttlecock on the lawn tomorrow?" Diana brushed cake crumbs from her muslin skirt.

Dismounting, Toby sat down on the patched wing chair beside the low table. He piled his plate high with everything on offer. "We haven't played for ages. Why now?"

"I have a yen for it," Diana replied.

Toby's freckled nose twitched, reminding Helen of one of those inquisitive red squirrels in the park. "I remember you saying it was unladylike to launch yourself around the grass after you'd turned seventeen, Diana."

"Well, I'm eighteen in two weeks and much more

mature. A lady can change her mind."

"Tomorrow then. After breakfast." He took the teacup and saucer from Helen. "I'll have to make do with you for entertainment, I suppose, now that my Eton pals have gone off to the country."

"Fool!" Diana grinned, leaned across, and poked his arm. "Not after breakfast. Helen and I have an appointment with the dancing master and after that a French lesson. About three o'clock."

Eyebrows lifted, Toby looked from Helen to Diana. "I suspect an ulterior motive."

Diana dissected her cake with her fork. "We have little enough to do while Papa is engulfed in the depths of some Eastern library. He won't return for weeks. And there's a mystery to be solved."

"A mystery?" Toby turned to Helen. "What's afoot? Has Diana been reading one of Papa's books on Ancient Greece?" He gave an exaggerated shudder. "Or, worse, Mama's Gothic novels?"

"You'd best tell him, Diana." Helen rose to add hot water to the brown china teapot from the decorative gold and white samovar their father had brought back from his travels in Russia.

Diana frowned. "As you well know, I don't read Greek. That's a privilege only available to you and Harry."

"I doubt Harry is interested in ancient history while discovering the joys of Paris." Toby wrinkled his nose again. "You can attend my lessons for me, anytime. Well? Are you going to tell me about this mystery or not?"

"It's merely an instinct. There's not much to tell." Diana described the intriguing gentleman she'd been watching in the park. "This is the third time he's been there."

"I say!" Toby jumped up, rushed to the window, and threw up the sash. "No one down there now. Anyway, there are always people strolling the Queen's Walk to the Queen's Basin and back again. Queen Caroline had that reservoir built to provide water for St. James's. She had the library erected too."

"Heaven knows what will happen to them now. It's said that the king wishes to divorce her," Helen said.

"Well, the gentleman disappeared from the park some time ago. A good thing too." Diana gave a huff of disgust. "You're so mutton-headed you would have scared him off. You'd make a dreadful spy, I must say. But he's the reason we need to be down there tomorrow. If he comes again, we can confront him."

"What if he's a thief working out how he can break in and rob us?"

"He's not."

"How do you know that?" Toby asked, his mouth full of ham sandwich.

"He's too well dressed to be a thief."

"Well, if he is a rook, I'll plant him a facer!"

"My goodness, Toby. As if you could!" Helen said with a huff of dismay. "Your imagination is worse than Diana's."

The door opened, and the nanny came in, holding the hand of their young brother. "Here is Lord Alexander, Lady

Helen. If you could just watch him for an hour until milady returns from the lending library."

"Please give our best wishes to your mother, Miss Prince," Helen said. "I hope you find her in better health."

When Diana and Toby added their best wishes to Helen's, Miss Prince smiled. "Thank you. I must hurry or I'll have little time to spend with Mother. And I plan to buy her some of those wonderful scotch eggs Fortnum and Masons make."

As the door closed, Helen opened her arms. With a joyful cry, the chubby four-year-old boy climbed into her lap. She stroked his copper curls as he struggled to reach the food on the table. "You may have a sandwich and a slice of cake, Zander. I'll be in trouble if you don't eat your dinner."

"Thank you, Helen," Alexander said in his endearing baby voice. He took the sandwich and slid off her lap to investigate the toy chest in the corner.

"Do you intend to find a husband this Season, Helen?" Toby asked with his usual lack of tact.

"My goodness no. It's Diana's debut. I don't intend to marry."

"Oh, but you must, Helen," Diana said.

"Not every woman must."

Helen looked away from Diana's concerned gaze. After her own Season ended in disaster some years ago, she'd reluctantly come to London and endured hot crammed ballrooms, Almack's dances designed to marry one off, and horrid routs, while missing Bertie, her dog, and the beautiful spring at Cherrywood, their country home. She supposed at twenty-four she was fast becoming a spinster, but it ceased to worry her now that she had decided what her future would be. It lay ahead, soothing her as she tidied up the cake crumbs.

Diana gave a puzzled frown. "You seem to want so little from life, Helen. I remember how your first Season ended so regrettably, but you have discouraged several suitors since then. You would make a wonderful mother. Unlike me. Father says I'm adventurous while Mama accuses me of being too impetuous."

"I'm sure they're both right," Toby said, leaping in with both feet and receiving a sharp poke in the side from Diana.

~~~

Jason, Captain, Lord Peyton, strode away through the trees of the park, a muscle tightening in his jaw. Still no sign of his informant. Had he met with foul play? If the man failed to turn up tomorrow, Jason would return to Whitehall and consult Lord Parnell, the Spymaster General, who'd pressured him to take this job. Jason hadn't been involved in intelligence work since the Peninsular War, and he had little inclination to do more of it, but Parnell could be forceful, and even quite ruthless. He was not to be denied once he'd considered Jason best suited to investigate a member of the upper classes without detection.

Already an extremely reluctant participant in what seemed a hastily conjured-up mission, Jason had better things to do with his time than kicking his heels up in the park. Why his contact hadn't suggested somewhere more discreet he didn't know. A pub in the Seven Dials would have been wiser. Here, these big free-standing mansions along the Queen's Walk would overlook them. For all he knew, he could have had a dozen curious eyes on him while he waited there. In fact, he'd caught sight of a fiery head at one of the upper-story windows. But that would most likely be a maid or a child in the nursery.

Details of their information were sketchy at best. Only that the informant was employed in one of the houses along the Walk. The arrangement was for the man to slip out and divulge some threat he'd uncovered that the government decided merited close examination. But where was he? Had it been a ruse? The man had asked particularly for Jason, whom he said he trusted. But Jason didn't even know what position he held or from which of those big houses he came. It irked him to be so ill informed. As he only had the briefest connection to one or two of the inhabitants, Parnell would need to produce a viable reason for Jason to visit them.

Twenty minutes later, he entered his Mayfair townhouse in South Audley Street and relinquished his coat, hat, cane, and gloves into the arms of his butler, Russell.

"The post has come, my lord."

Jason removed his mail from the silver salver on the pier table and headed up the sweep of stairs to the upper floors, scanning a scrawled missive from his brother, Charlie, up at Oxford. What scrape was he in now? Money, he supposed. It usually was.

His sister, Lizzie, appeared at the banister rail on the landing above him, her dark hair covered by a white lace cap tied at an angle under her chin. She'd forgone her widow weeds for half-mourning and wore a gray dress with bands of purple on the collar, hem, and cuffs.

"Jason, would you care to escort me to the Peckworths' soiree this evening?"

"I'd be delighted." He was pleased and somewhat relieved when Lizzie had come to London to stay with him, revealing an interest in Society again. He examined his sister's peaky face. In contrast to her black hair, her skin was like alabaster. But the bruised look beneath her eyes, evidence of her profound sadness, had faded. Greywood had been gone for more than eighteen months. It was time to take her place in society again.

On the following afternoon, Jason took up his position in the park. Breathing in the smell of sun-drenched grasses, he leaned against a tree and pulled his younger brother's letter from his pocket. Charlie was being sent down for some misdemeanor or other. He'd explain when he arrived. Jason still was unable to discern much from the hasty lines. How serious was it? Worse than the time he'd put itching powder in his tutor's linen? Or when he'd missed a whole afternoon of lectures to take part in a rowing race on the Isis near Folly Bridge? The fact that he was the finest rower they'd had for years got him out of that one. This one might not be so easy. There was something final behind his words.

Again, no one approached Jason to identify himself. He studied his pocket watch and, with an annoyed shake of his head, returned it to his waistcoat pocket deciding to remain for only fifteen minutes more.

A dark-haired woman in a brown pelisse and straw bonnet, with a basket over her arm, cast him a sharp, inquiring look before entering the garden gate of the mansion in front of him. After greeting a young woman and a youth playing shuttlecock, she paused in conversation with a gardener raking leaves at the far corner of the lawn then disappeared through the servants' door.

The young woman with curls the color of a copper pan caught Jason's attention. She squealed and hit the shuttlecock over the net then stopped to look his way, as if seeking his praise.

Jason smiled and applauded.

The young gentleman, who was no more than fifteen, turned then, and Jason saw this as his chance.

He removed his hat and crossed the walk to their gate. "Lord Peyton. Good day to you."

The pair dropped their bats and hurried over to him. Two pairs of intense blue eyes studied him. "We've seen you here before, my lord. May we be of help?" The young woman smiled. She was pretty, her bright curls coiled about her small ears beneath her bonnet. Had she been watching him from one of the upper-story windows yesterday?

Her blue eyes sparkled. "Were you waiting for someone? A lady perhaps?"

Startled, Jason clamped his lips down on a laugh. "I'm afraid not. Purely business. I'm from the Office of Works.

I'm sure you're aware that John Nash is renovating Buckingham Palace for the King, as well as Green Park."

The boy opened the gate and stepped through. He offered his hand. "How do you do? I am Tobias Kinsey, and this is my sister, Lady Diana."

Jason shook his hand. "Your father is Lawrence Kinsey, the scholar and explorer?"

"You've heard of him?" Lady Diana asked. "I suppose we shouldn't be surprised. Father's work is well known."

"We have met." Jason recalled Lord Kinsey drawing him into conversation about the need for funding for some research trip at a dinner. Had all his children inherited his periwinkle blue eyes? Arresting in Lawrence Kinsey's suntanned face when he'd aimed his forceful gaze at Jason and begged assistance. Jason had given it without hesitation. Such was the charm of the man. The elder son of the Marquess of Walcott, Kinsey was known to be brilliant if unconventional.

"Father is away at present," Lord Tobias explained. "Would you like to come for tea? We love visitors."

"Thank you. I'll be pleased to call when your father returns."

"Our mother is at home. Please do come," Lord Tobias said with a surprising eagerness. "I'd like to learn more about the renovations to the park."

"We are most dreadfully short of company," Lady Diana added, distracting Jason with her dimples.

Smiling, Jason reached into his coat pocket. "We can't have that, now can we? I'll call tomorrow at two if it's convenient." He handed Lord Tobias his card with his name and address printed on it in silver script.

"Is that the man you wished to see?" Lady Diana asked, pointing.

Jason twisted and caught sight of the back of a dark-haired man walking away through the park. "No. It appears the man I was to meet has been held up yet again." He bowed. "Enjoy your game."

"I know my sister, Helen, would like to meet you," Lady Diana called after him.

He replaced his hat and, with a grin, paced along the path through the trees. The name Diana, that of the mythological Roman goddess of the hunt, the moon, and nature, quite suited the slender young woman, who had displayed athletic grace playing shuttlecock. Tobias was also an ancient Greek name, Jason recalled with amusement. And might Helen be as beautiful as Helen of Troy, daughter of Zeus and Leda? Whether she was or not, he suspected the whole family would have an abundance of charm.

As he tossed a coin to the crossing-sweeper at Piccadilly, his thoughts returned to the failure of his contact to appear. Was it in the Kinsey house that the informant had discovered some plot against the Crown? Lord Kinsey was eccentric, but he was said to be an honorable man. His obsession with ancient texts and tombs could make him vulnerable to the crafty and unscrupulous, however. Jason would be loath to uncover something unsavory within those walls. Where was the missing informant? Why had his letter been so annoyingly obscure? This might not be as easy a mission as Parnell suggested.

Damn, it was a bad time for Charlie to make an appearance.

CHAPTER TWO

When Mary laid out Helen's floral cambric, Diana gave a moue of distaste. "Why don't you wear your lilac sarsnet? It makes your eyes look mysterious."

In her chemise, stays, and petticoats, Helen turned to her with a sigh. "It's afternoon tea, not a soirée."

Diana's golden eyebrows drew together in an exasperated frown. "That's no reason for you not to look your best."

"The gentleman is not coming to see me," Helen said. "You look so pretty in that primrose muslin, Diana, I doubt he'll notice me at all."

"Mama has met Lord Peyton. He served under Wellington and is over thirty."

Helen smiled wryly. "Too old for you, then."

Diana gave a carefree shrug. "Debutantes often marry much older gentlemen."

When the maid finished fastening the hooks down Helen's back and stepped away, Helen smoothed the high-necked collar of the cream, brown, and gray patterned dress before the mirror then, leaning closely, tweaked a curl beside her ear to better hide the scar. They were to receive several callers this afternoon. Lady Moncrieff and her daughter, Charlotte, who she was launching this Season, and the Baker twins, whose mother always reminisced about the success of her own Season many years ago.

Helen tamped down a yearning for the country in spring, as she did every Season. She had to steel herself, aware that they would be inundated with invitations once everyone returned to the city. She ruthlessly banished the idyllic dream of rolling green hills dotted with daisies and black and white cows. She would remain in London and attend a dozen Almack's dances if need be to see Diana married to the love of her life. "Shall we go down?"

"I am looking forward to seeing Peyton again," Diana said as they descended the stairs together. "I know you will approve of him."

Helen laughed. "How can you be sure on such short acquaintance?"

"Well, he has the most wonderful dark green eyes, but there's much more to him than that, as you'll see."

"Not that old dress, Helen!" Mama sighed as she swept down the staircase behind them, the hem of her claret-colored gown raised in one slender hand. With her tall slim figure and long neck, their mother was always graceful. And Father adored her. Helen had once hoped that a man would feel that way about her. But four Seasons on from her first introduction to the *ton*, she no longer considered it possible.

She was forced to accept that, although she'd been born

into a family of striking good looks, hers were passable at best. She'd inherited her mother's abundant chestnut hair and gray eyes, but not her tall, willowy frame. And none of her vivacity. Helen knew she lacked countenance. She was like a small gray dove amongst a batch of showy peacocks. The only time she had reached for the moon it had ended in disaster. She was extremely unlikely to ever do it again.

At a quarter to two, their butler, Fiske, showed Lord Peyton, into the drawing room carrying a valise. Seen at close quarters, he was indeed handsome, with a tall lithe figure and disordered ebony curls that rejected his large hand's attempt to tame them. Immaculate in a marine blue tailcoat, thigh-tight fawn trousers, and a patterned cream silk waistcoat with etched silver buttons, his lengthy stride took him smartly across the carpet's swirls of pink and gold to where Helen, her mother, Diana, and Toby, had risen from the twin sofas beside the fireplace.

"Lord Peyton, how good to see you again," Mama said. "May I introduce you to my children?"

"I have already had the pleasure of meeting two of them." He smiled at Diana and Toby. "Forgive me for being a little early. I wanted to see you before the rush of afternoon callers."

"You are forgiven, my lord." With a smile, Mama placed a gentle hand on Helen's shoulder, giving her the tiniest push. "I don't believe you've met my eldest daughter, Lady Helen."

"No, indeed." Observant dark green eyes flecked with

gold and fringed with dark lashes acknowledged Helen from beneath straight jet-black brows. He bowed. "How do you do."

"My lord." Maddeningly, Helen felt herself blush as she curtseyed. Diana was right; he was uncommonly handsome. But more disturbingly, there was a wealth of experience in those eyes.

"I must beg your forgiveness, Lord Peyton. We are at sixes and sevens here with Bartholomew, our footman, and a kitchen boy both taken to their beds with a malaise, and Bartholomew," Mama explained, "remains quite ill." She gestured to the adjacent upholstered chair. "I have ordered tea. Or would you care for wine?"

"Tea would be most welcome, thank you." He sat and crossed his long legs. "It is good of you to see me with his lordship away. As you will be aware, there are considerable alterations to be made to Green Park and its environs. I have been sent to explain the process to those who will be most affected."

"But not to hear our objections?" Mama asked.

A smile tugged at his lips, revealing white teeth. "Mr. Nash appreciates honesty."

"Of that, I have some doubt." Mama returned his smile. "I have met Mr. Nash, a remarkable architect who would have scant desire for my opinion. However, I am keen to see what you have brought."

Jeremy, their sole footman at present, entered with a maid and began unloading the tea trays onto the low table. Helen automatically rose to assist them. She presided over the silver teapot on its warming stand.

"I shall pour while you peruse his lordship's papers, Mama." Her mother had reluctantly relinquished the task to her, with the proviso that Helen need not expect to continue the practice as the family spinster.

"If you'll permit me." Lord Peyton moved a side table closer to her mother. He opened his valise and removed several drawings.

Toby left his seat for a closer look. "I say, sir, garden design is an interest of mine. I am a great admirer of Capability Brown. Grandfather employed him for the gardens at Walcott, and they are regarded as being amongst the best in England."

Lord Peyton smiled. "Ah yes, Lord Tobias, Lancelot Brown did indeed create some very fine gardens. I should appreciate your thoughts on these."

Unrolling the plans, he spread them out over the table. "As you can see there will be a large planting of trees."

Toby leaned over them. "Will the temples and the library remain?"

"For the present," Lord Peyton said.

Toby launched into a discussion of the hated return of geometric-styled gardens, reinforcing his argument with references to Virgil and the idyllic images of the Roman Campagna, depicted by the seventeenth-century French landscape painter Claude Lorrain.

Not wishing to distract her brother, but taking pity on the earl, Helen offered him the plate of dainty ham and cress sandwiches. He added several to his plate with a polite nod then turned back to Toby, who had moved on to the literature of Pope to support his view.

"I believe enough has been said about the previous century, Toby." Mama smiled at him. "We must move forward."

"It all looks quite wonderful!" Diana said breathlessly and fluttered her lashes at his lordship.

"And you, Lady Helen?" Lord Peyton turned to her.

Coming under his scrutiny, Helen caught her breath at the force of his masculinity. His olive skin was lightly sunburned. Not one of those gentlemen who favored the night and slept past noon, perhaps. There was a faint ray of lines at the corners of his eyes as if he smiled a lot. But the harsh set to his angular jaw and his firm mouth discounted any assessment of softness in his character. His delay in seeking them out had not been explained to her satisfaction. "I hope the man you sought in the park finally appeared, my lord?"

"Not as yet."

Did he think her inquisitive? "The trees appeal to me. Especially the varied species," she said, hastily answering his question. "I greatly admire my grandfather's gardens. And we have a splendid variety of trees at Cherrywood."

Distracting herself, she added more hot water to the pot as her mother drew his lordship into conversation. Peyton certainly could be charming and had her mother laughing at something he'd read about King George's stables in Brighton. It was stated that the horses in their heated stables were far more comfortable than the guests. Then, when Toby seized an opportunity to draw him back to a discussion of gardens, she liked that Peyton patiently listened and agreed.

Diana was enamored of him, and eyeing the breadth of Lord Peyton's shoulders, Helen could quite see why. Was she being too suspicious? He did have a valid reason to come and discuss the proposal for Green Park. And it might well be that Diana's beauty had drawn him here. No doubt the first of many gentlemen to call once the Season began.

~~~

Jason returned the plans that Parnell had procured for him to his valise. Plans that gave him an introduction to every house along the Queen's Walk. However, he would have to become more inventive if he were to discover what lay behind this latest threat to English security.

He glanced into Lady Helen's large gray eyes and, seizing the silver tongs, took a lump of sugar from the bowl she offered him. Not a great beauty like Helen of Troy, but a curvaceous young woman with a very kissable plump Cupid's-bow mouth. She favored neither of her tall parents. She had an air of quiet reserve, but he suspected she missed little. He enjoyed watching her neat movements as she presided over the tea tray, finding it oddly soothing.

He stirred his tea and smiled at his hostess. "Lord Kinsey will need to view these. When might he be expected home?"

"My husband has been visiting Alexandria. We hope to

see him toward the end of next week. I shall advise his secretary to notify you when he has arrived."

"Thank you." Having finished his tea, Jason rose to take his leave.

"It was so good of you to call." Lady Diana curtseyed prettily and favored him with another dimpled smile while her sister nodded in polite if less effusive agreement.

Jason bowed and left the room, amused. Lady Diana would do well in her first Season.

Lord Tobias followed him down the passage to the front door, picking up his conversation where he'd left off, listing famous gardens of note.

"Mr. John Nash is a proponent of the picturesque in architecture. Have you met him, Lord Tobias?"

The lad tapped his chin, giving the unlikely event due consideration. "No, I don't believe I have."

"And should you like to?" Jason felt confident that Nash, who he knew quite well, would welcome a youngster's interest in his work.

"Oh, yes. I most certainly would, sir…" His eagerness faded, and an expression of dismay crossed his face. "Father would be unlikely to permit it. I am told that I must concentrate on my studies. Especially Latin and Greek, although I doubt they'll be of much help to me once my schooling is behind me."

With a nod, Jason took his hat, cane, and gloves from the butler. "They proved most advantageous for your father, did they not? And your grand tour will be greatly enriched by that knowledge."

Jason kept his tongue firmly in his cheek. His grand tour had been spent with a group of young men who named their aged tutor Dozy because he would fall asleep at the drop of a hat, and once free of restraint, their tour had become more of a bacchanalian. He doubted the so-called cultural experience had taught him much at all, except perhaps how to drink until dawn and better pleasure a woman. His years in the army had taught him far more about life while bivouacking in camps on the march, reconnoitering behind enemy lines, or riding into battle with the acceptance that he might not see another day.

"I don't intend to follow in my father's footsteps." Lord Tobias leaned against the wall beside a marble statue of a partially dressed Roman goddess. "I have no wish to become a scholar," he said earnestly, seemingly unaffected by the marble breast at his elbow. "And as I won't have an estate to occupy my time, as Hector, my older brother—we call him Harry— is to inherit, life would be fearfully dull. That's why I intend to design houses and gardens. So you see, sir," Lord Tobias implored, "A meeting with Mr. Nash may be just the ticket."

"Perhaps, but you will need to work hard at mathematics," Jason said as the butler, with a wearisome glance at Tobias, opened the front door.

"Well, yes, I imagine so," Lord Tobias said, crestfallen. He brightened. "But you will try to arrange that meeting with Mr. Nash? I should be most grateful."

"I will do my best. But only if your parents agree."

Jason settled his hat on his head and walked out into the fragile spring sunshine. He'd had little success at two other mansions along the Walk, discounting them outright. Nor had anyone or anything alerted him to a possible plot being brewed within the Kinsey's walls, although he'd hardly expected the informant to approach him while he was taking tea. It was a masterstroke of Parnell's, getting Jason to do Nash's job of advising the households of the changes to the district. But none of this sat well with him. He was used to facing logistical problems in the army, where he could formulate a clear plan. Here, it seemed he wandered through a particularly perplexing maze.

The Kinseys had proved to be every bit as appealing as he'd expected. He found it surprising that Lady Helen of the distrustful gray eyes had not yet married. Surely many would have been tempted by a comely lady with a good dowry. Despite her attempts to hide her attractiveness beneath a high-necked gown adorned with a simple cameo brooch and behaving like a maiden aunt at surely no more than twenty-two or three. The dress failed to disguise a youthful and alluring figure, and there was no way she could hide her fine eyes and that rosebud mouth. There was a story here. As he walked back home, he allowed his mind to dwell on that more appealing mystery.

CHAPTER THREE

"Well? What did you think of Lord Peyton?" Diana asked Helen as Jeremy seated them at the dining table.

Helen couldn't help smiling at her sister's eager question but could offer no clear opinion of the earl. "You were right about his handsome looks. He's as elegantly dressed as a dandy. But I doubt he is like any of the Bond Street beaus."

Diana raised her eyebrows. "Why?"

"Just an impression." In her first Season, Helen had detested finding herself the subject of discussion by a band of dandies whenever she shopped and attended balls. "I can't imagine Peyton ogling women while considering their potential as wives."

Diana shrugged. "I shouldn't mind if he ogled me. I'm not like you, Helen. I'm comfortable at the center of attention. And I don't see why you think he's so very different from other men. He will surely want to marry like all men in need of an heir."

"What Helen means, my dear, is that you could not easily wrap Lord Peyton around your little finger, as you might do with some young blades," Mama said as she was seated.

Diana's eyes flashed. "I love a challenge."

"Your father would not approve of him for you. I fear you'll be hurt." She nodded to the butler who waited to serve claret from the decanter while Jeremy and the maids brought in the first course under silver covers, filling the dining room with delicious aromas.

Steam coiled from the cream of cauliflower soup placed before her. Helen picked up her spoon. "Perhaps it's his lordship's experiences during the war. He is nothing like Lord Falkingham, who smiles beguilingly and hangs on Diana's every word whenever he comes to see Papa."

"Falkingham is a fop." Diana sighed. "Peyton is very masculine."

"My dear love, you will have your pick of prospective husbands at your come-out ball," Mama said. "Choose a man who will deal gently with you. A man who does not understand you might crush your spirit."

"That sounds as if you don't like Lord Peyton." Diana served herself some halibut. "He is very approachable and exhibits none of the *froideur* so fashionable amongst the dandies."

"No, he was not cold or aloof in his manner, in fact, I found him quite amiable. Nevertheless, there is steel beneath. You also are of a determined nature, Diana. You have been thus since you were a baby. But some men will not easily bend to your will."

"Lord Peyton—" Diana began.

Mama held up a graceful hand. "Men like Peyton, who was an officer during the most brutal campaigns fighting Napoleon, are not biddable."

"But what if such a man falls in love?" Helen asked. That could change most men she imagined.

"Perhaps then. With the right woman." Mama glanced at Helen. "A sensible wife could make all the difference. Especially one who has had some experience of life." She patted Diana's arm. "But not a girl just out of the schoolroom."

Diana bristled. "I am almost eighteen, Mama."

"And your father has kept you carefully sheltered within the bosom of this family." Mama smiled. "I agree that it is time for you to spread your wings. But I want you to enjoy your first Season. It is the most wonderful time of your life; do not waste it chasing after rainbows. Meet many gentlemen, and choose the best one for your husband."

After dinner, once Helen and Diana dismissed their maid and climbed into bed, Diana folded her arms over the coverlet. "I don't think Mama gives me enough credit."

"You know Mama is far wiser than we are, Diana."

"Normally, I would agree. I am no longer a child, and she needs to realize that. But she soon will."

Recognizing the defiant note in Diana's voice, Helen rolled over to study her sister in the flickering light. "As Mama said, many men will attend your ball who are of a suitable age and disposition."

"I expected such a sensible reply from you, Helen."

Diana yawned. "You don't have my passion for life. I can't imagine you falling madly in love with someone entirely unsuitable. Blow out the candle, will you? I'm sleepy."

She supposed Diana was right. Helen rubbed her arms and lay staring into the dark. She well understood her sister's attraction to Lord Peyton. She, too, had noticed his strength and confidence, but Helen had also detected a world-weariness in his eyes. She foresaw trouble ahead. Papa had always told Diana she could have anything in life she wished for. In Helen's experience, it was a man's world, and that was unlikely to change, for men controlled every aspect of a woman's life.

She knew that Papa had hoped for one of his children to follow in his footsteps and share his work. Neither Toby nor their elder brother, Harry, were interested. And why should Harry be? His letters were filled with new discoveries on the Continent, and he would one day inherit Papa's estate and a tidy fortune. Their father had some years ago concluded, somewhat unfairly, that Helen, or Hedgehog, as he affectionately called her, an animal who curled up into a ball when upset, would not be his chosen companion. And as Alexander was still a baby, that left Diana, who resembled him most in personality. Unfortunately, Helen suspected her sister's show of interest in ancient works generally coincided with something Mama had refused her, which Papa inevitably agreed to.

~~~

Jason realized Charlie had arrived home as soon as he

put a foot in the door. Russell's face split into a smile as he directed Jason to the kitchen. The sound of laughter emanated from below as Jason descended the stairs. Laughter had not been heard in this house for some time. He paused with a hand on the banister, realizing how much he had missed it.

Jason continued down the stairs. All very well, but Charlie required a strong hand, and before their father died, he had promised he'd see his scamp of a brother safely into adulthood.

Charlie sat at the scrubbed table, flirting outrageously with the kitchen maid while Cook placed before him a plate of thickly sliced ham, bread and butter, and a slab of fruit cake. The kitchen maid, who had been hanging on Charlie's every word, caught sight of Jason, and turned red.

Charlie pushed back his chair and jumped up. "Jas! I was hoping I'd see you before I went out." He thumped Jason's back and enveloped him in a hug.

Jason grinned despite himself. "It is good to see you, Charlie." He forced his features into a stern expression as he joined him at the table and picked up a piece of ham from his plate. Swallowing the tasty ham, he accepted a good strong cup of tea from Cook. "A pity it's under such distressing circumstances. Where might you be dashing off to?"

"Came down on a stage coach. Met a fellow who's going to the cockfights. Thought I might join him."

At that, Jason tossed back the tea and put down the cup.

"Finish up your food and then join me in the library, will you?" He climbed to his feet.

"Yes, of course, Jas. I believe I have time before—"

"And allow Molly to get on with her work."

The girl flushed again and bowed her head over the peas she was shelling.

"Forgive me, milord." Cook anxiously pleated her apron. "It's just that I haven't seen Mister Charles since last year when we was all back at Peyton Grove."

Jason smiled. "Perfectly understandable, Cook. You have known my rascal brother since he was a lad. Of course, you enjoy seeing him again. As do I."

He returned upstairs, thinking that Charlie could charm anyone in skirts, even the fearsome Mrs. Newbold, their housekeeper, who would no doubt soon succumb. But where was their sister?

When he tapped on Lizzie's door, her maid opened it. "Lady Greywood is walking in the park with a gentleman, milord."

"Which gentleman, Sally?" he asked in surprise. "And why didn't you accompany her?"

"As it was merely a short stroll, my lord, my presence was not required." The tone of her voice revealed her disapproval. Sally had been Lizzie's lady's maid when her beloved husband, Greywood, had suffered a mortal wound during a shooting accident. Since then Sally had become most protective of her. The maid hurried over to the dressing table and picked up a card, returning to hand it to him.

He glanced at the bold black script. "Who is this Baron Antonio Bianchi?"

"Her ladyship met him at the Covent Garden opera two nights ago. Lady Plummer introduced them."

"I see." Jason didn't see at all. Since she'd come to London, Lizzie had repelled two highly suitable suitors. Jason had put that down to Greywood. Any man would find it difficult to measure up to her memories of her deceased husband. Admittedly, his sister was no green girl at twenty-five, but she was vulnerable, and he'd protect her from hurt at any cost. He would find out more about this baron when she returned, but first, he had to talk to Charlie.

As he returned to the library, it occurred to him that he should get his own household in order before he tried to delve into other people's lives. Damn Parnell, why couldn't he leave him alone? The spymaster had stated flatly that he considered Jason to be sleepwalking through life since the war, and as he knew the reason why, Jason had no defense.

"If you'd set up your nursery I wouldn't ask this of you, but rusticating in the country isn't the life for any red-blooded male. And certainly not for one of Wellington's finest spies. I, and Wellington, had expected you to go on to bigger things."

Parnell had continued ruthlessly, using his talent for persuasion while insinuating he was doing Jason a favor to shake him out of his lethargy. "The informant fears for his life and has chosen not to divulge any details concerning his own situation or his name. But he asked particularly for you.

A man he said he can trust."

Jason had no idea who that could be.

"This will neither be a difficult mission, nor a long one," Parnell had assured him. "Just a few inquiries and Whitehall will take it from there. And I know you wouldn't wish to leave me in the lurch, knowing how shorthanded we are with our best men away from England."

Sleepwalking through life? Parnell was wrong there. Upon inheriting the title of earl, Jason gained an estate in Surrey along with this Mayfair townhouse and some solid investments, which paid the bills. Parnell was right about one thing. He did not intend to marry and inflict his moods on any hapless woman, and he was not interested in setting up a permanent mistress after Genevieve, who had proved to be every bit as demanding as any wife.

It was a comfortable existence, and he saw no reason to change it. He preferred to be at Peyton Grove, working with his steward to improve the estate and visiting his tenants. The rhythm of country-life suited him. And after years in the army, he preferred a busy active life. No lady would ever agree to such a dull existence. She would rightly want to come to London for the Season. And except for the cut and thrust of the House of Lords, the company of a few friends, or to visit a lady, London society didn't hold a great deal of charm for him. He was only here now for Lizzie's sake.

Jason found his brother stalking up and down the richly patterned Turkey carpet in the library. Charlie swung around. "I only have a few minutes, Jas. I have to keep a promise, as I've mentioned."

Jason gestured to a wingchair, and his brother collapsed his lanky frame onto it. "What on earth happened? Why have you been sent down?"

Charlie's green-eyed gaze dropped away, and he rubbed his chin. "I was discovered with a woman in my quarters."

Drawing in a deep breath, Jason sought the leather chair at his desk. He tapped an irritated finger on the tooled leather desktop. "Devil take it! You know the rules, Charlie. And you've flouted them once too often."

Charlie had the grace to look shamefaced. "It was a rescue mission, Jas. Didn't turn out that way, though."

"A rescue mission?"

"A young lady, Miss Amelia Groton, needed help. A friend of mine, Basil Wentworth, arranged to meet her in my rooms, to assist her, but someone tipped off the dean."

"Why couldn't he damned well meet her in his own rooms?"

"Because his roommate, Bosky Bellows, had come down with some nasty contagious malaise."

Jason gritted his teeth. "Has your chum, so-called, been to the dean and confessed all?"

Charlie nodded gloomily. "He's also been sent down."

"Well, that's a nice kettle of fish."

"I can't see the dean taking me back, Jas. But look on the bright side. I can keep you and Lizzie company. I'll just need some transport. I thought a high-top phaeton. It will need to be yellow, too, as I thought I might join—"

"Stop right there." Glaring at his young brother, Jason

had begun to feel every year of his age and more.

Charlie slumped and fiddled with his cravat. "I'm sorry I've disappointed you."

"It's not a matter of disappointing me. It's a matter of disappointing yourself, Charlie. You are almost twenty-one. You come into your inheritance at twenty-five, and then you can do what you damn well please. But until then I remain in charge. Do you understand?"

"Yes, Jas," Charlie mumbled. He stopped tugging his cravat and despoiled the artful arrangement of his black curls. "What will you do?"

"I'll write to some friends. I should be able to pull a few strings."

"I expect you will." Charlie's mouth pulled down at the corners. "I suppose I won't need the yellow carriage now, will I?"

"You will have one eventually. Good things come to those who wait."

"I'll be too old to enjoy it." Charlie climbed to his feet. "I don't suppose I could have some of the ready? I find myself at a stand after paying for the trip down from Oxford."

"I consider cockfighting to be a shabby way for a man to toss away his blunt, but I see it will be useless to dissuade you."

"I did promise, Jas."

"I shan't be subsidizing your allowance to pay for any gambling losses, so please try to keep your nose clean while here in London." Jason reached for his cash box. Unlocking it, he counted out ten pounds.

"Traveling is an expensive business." Charlie nodded his thanks and pocketed the money. "Especially if you have to escort a lady."

Jason raised his head from locking the box. "You brought a lady with you to London?"

"I need to tell you about that." Charlie was hurrying to the door. "I haven't time now. I'll explain later."

Jason watched the door shut behind his brother. "Why does Parnell think my life is boring?" he asked the empty room. He had yet to deal with his sister, and that would require far more tact. At least tact was completely lost on Charlie

CHAPTER FOUR

"A letter has arrived from your father." Mama entered the breakfast room, where Helen, Diana, and Toby sat at the table with the appetizing smells of eggs, bacon, and kippers from the hot dishes wafting from the sideboard.

Helen stopped buttering toast. "Is Papa on his way home?"

"I believe so. His letter was dated a month ago when he was soon to board the ship for England. He had just returned to Alexandria after visiting the Temple of Hathor at Dendera. He has confirmed a theory and remains confident his research is sound."

"Does he say what the theory is?" Having spread marmalade on her toast, Helen took a bite.

"He doesn't, dear. There's only so much room for your father's large cursive on the page, and he seemed to be in a rush. He sends his love and is eager to hug his loved ones again."

"How very like Papa," Diana said with a laugh. "To send us exciting news and not tell us what it is."

"We shall learn of it all in good time, Diana." Mama paused as Fiske entered the room to provide hot water.

Helen doubted they'd learn much more from Papa. When he was at home, he closeted himself in his library and didn't always see fit to tell them what took up so much of his time. But she longed to see him again. He had been gone for over two months, and their home just didn't feel right without him. "How is Bart today, Mama, and Jinx?"

Mama shook her head, her eyes sad. "I had not wished to discuss this with you until after breakfast. Jinx has recovered and returned to his duties in the kitchen. But our footman is very ill indeed. The doctor called again early this morning. Brace yourselves, my dears, Bartholomew is not expected to live for much longer."

"Oh, Mama!" Diana and Helen cried in unison.

"Poor Bart." Toby's voice wobbled with distress. He pushed away his half-eaten plate of bacon and eggs. "I went to see him yesterday, but was told he was sleeping."

"I shall visit him this morning," Mama said. "I hope to ask him what his last wishes might be. I'll consult Father's secretary when he arrives. Mr. Thorburn will need to deal with this matter in your father's absence."

"Can we say goodbye?" Helen asked with a sad wrench.

"If you really wish to, although it will be distressing, and I'm sure Bartholomew won't expect it."

"We want to, Mama," Toby said.

"Very well. The doctor assures me he is not infectious."

Helen glanced at her brother and sister while wiping

away a tear. Bart had been a part of their household for years. He had always impressed her with his ability to perform his duties perfectly with only one arm.

~~~

Lizzie brought the sweet fragrance of sunlit gardens into the library with her arms full of aromatic flowers. Her cheeks were flushed, and there was a sparkle he had not seen for some years in her eye. "How agreeable to find you at home, Jason. These are for my sitting room. I mean to borrow that pretty blue and white vase on the mantelpiece."

Jason rang for the footman as she unloaded the bunch onto a table. "Stay and talk to me," he said, seizing the opportunity to speak to her.

When the footman appeared, she gave him the vase and filled his arms with the pink and white blooms. "Please tell Sally to fill the vase with water, arrange the flowers, and set them in my sitting room, thank you, Henry.

"They're so gorgeous I couldn't resist buying them from a flower seller," she said after the footman departed.

"Indeed. I do hope Henry doesn't drop that urn. I believe it's Sèvres."

Jason disliked having to question her. But question her, he must. Greywood had left her very wealthy. Lizzie had been barely out of the schoolroom when she married in her first Season. She was of a trusting nature. Well, he was not. "You look very pleased with something, my dear. I doubt it's the flowers alone."

"Not entirely. A gentleman and I have had a pleasant

promenade in the park."

Jason shifted his shoulders. "Yes, Sally told me. I saw his calling card."

Lizzie's eyes widened. "Oh?"

Jason placed his compendium of Wordsworth poetry he read in his quiet moments on the side table. He was doubtful there'd be too many of those for a while as he turned in the wingchair to better view Lizzie on the sofa. "Who is this Baron Bianchi?"

"He has an estate in Florence. An ancient baronetcy. The baron is visiting London for a few months."

"Why has he come to England?"

She smoothed her gray skirts and fixed him with a determined gaze. "Does he need a reason?"

"A man generally does," Jason said gently.

"He is here on business." She shrugged. "I knew you would be suspicious!"

"I believe it to be prudent. Until the facts are before me."

She eyed him with a calculating expression. "You would not feel that way if he was an English gentleman."

"I'd be no less so. It's my duty to care for your interests, Lizzie." Greywood had wished it, although Jason didn't want to remind her of it. He rose and went to the drinks tray on the sideboard and poured himself a brandy. "A glass of Madeira? Or would you prefer me to ring for tea?"

"Madeira. I feel in need of some fortifying."

Jason laughed as he handed her the glass. "Do you think your older brother an ogre?"

She smiled. "Certainly not. A bit stuffy perhaps."

He arched an eyebrow. "I shall ignore that, as I suspect it's meant to distract me from my purpose." His grin slid away. "But why you feel the need for fortification does worry me a little."

She sighed. "Promise me you will meet him."

"I fully intend to."

"Then I shall invite him to dinner."

"Excellent notion." He returned to his chair and crossed his legs. "However, there's no reason why you can't tell me more about him in the interim."

She sipped from her glass. "Bianchi is about your age, has never married, and, like me, is interested in Italian Renaissance art. He is handsome and good company. Will that suit?"

"It's a beginning. Why has he never married?"

"One might ask you the same question."

Jason shook his head. "We are discussing this new swain of yours." He would be deeply pleased to see the change in his sister, if only he could be sure the man merited it.

"He told me he planned to marry, but his fiancée died. It broke his heart." She gave a heavy sigh. "So you see, we have much in common."

A common interest in art and a broken heart seemed a tad too convenient. Jason suspected the situation could become challenging. He returned her smile and took a deep gulp of brandy. This would need to be settled before he was called back to the Queen's Walk on Kinsey's return. "Send Henry with a message. Invite the baron to dinner this evening."

"I'm sure he will be grateful. This is his first trip to England and he knows very few people here. But it will put poor Cook in a flap."

He laughed. "Cook complains that I don't entertain enough. I'll send her notice, but I'm sure she is in the process of creating a feast for Charlie."

Lizzie giggled. "You may be right."

When Lizzie left the library, Jason glanced at the book beside him. He made no attempt to pick it up, knowing his attempt to read would be useless. It was bittersweet to watch Lizzie awaken to life. If only he could be sure of the man responsible for it.

Charlie wandered into Jason's dressing room some hours later while his batman come valet was adjusting his cravat.

"Damned if I can tie it the way you do, Hicks."

"It's your Adam's apple, my lord. It tends to spoil the arrangement."

"What would you have me do about it? Cut it off?"

Hicks chuckled. No, my lord, it's only when you tie the cravat yourself."

"A sneakier means with which to safeguard your position as my valet, I've never heard," Jason said with a roar of laughter.

Hicks fought a grin as he took up the clothes brush.

"Why so glum, Charlie?" Jason asked, eyeing him in the mirror.

"That cockfight turned out to be a poor show, hardly worth the effort." Charlie threw himself onto a chair. "Probably rigged."

And he lost his money, Jason surmised. A salient lesson, he hoped. "You need to hurry to change for dinner. We have a guest."

"Who is it?"

"A gentleman Lizzie has invited. A Baron Bianchi."

"Oh? Actually, I've invited two guests myself."

Jason frowned. "Have you notified Cook?"

"Yes, just been down to the kitchen. She's prepared enough to feed a troop."

"I'm sure she has," Jason said dryly. "Who are your guests?"

"Miss Groton, the lady I escorted from Oxford. She is staying with her aunt. The aunt is accompanying her."

"Is Miss Groton the sort of woman you would introduce to your sister?"

Charlie looked affronted. "Of course. There is nothing about her demeanor to offend."

Jason arched an eyebrow. "Then we shall have quite an interesting dinner party." He did up the cloth buttons of his single-breasted waistcoat embroidered with gold thread then nodded to his valet. "Thank you, Hicks. After you've assisted Charlie, you may have your dinner."

"Certainly, my lord." Hicks hurried out the door.

Jason pulled down his cuffs. "Now. While you dress, you can explain about Miss Groton."

Following his brother along the passage, Jason was

congratulating himself on remaining calm under the constant barrage of surprises his siblings inflicted on him when Charlie paused at the door.

"There's something I need to get off my chest, Jas. I told Miss Groton you could help her out of her predicament."

"I can hardly wait to learn of it," Jason said wearily.

"I think I'll wear my new Apollo gold waistcoat tonight. It won't clash with yours," Charlie said, entering his bedroom.

"Tell me one thing," Jason said following him. "Where is this Basil Wentworth who got you into this scrape? And why isn't he assisting Miss Groton?"

"He's returned home to his family in Yorkshire. His father isn't plump in the pocket, and so I volunteered to deal with the problem."

"Shall you wear the navy wool coat with the velvet collar, sir? It complements the gold waistcoat," Hicks inquired, the coat over his arm.

"Perfect choice, Hicks. Well done." Charlie stripped off his coat. "I suppose I should shave." He ran a hand over his relatively smooth chin.

"No time for that." Jason straddled the ribbon-back wooden chair. He leaned his arm on the top, watching his brother. He wondered what lay behind this latest incident that Charlie didn't wish to tell him. "Please continue."

"It's just that Miss Groton" — Charlie's voice was muffled as he pulled his shirt up over his head — "has been the recipient of some cruel treatment," he finished as he reemerged.

"There's a basin of hot water and soap on the dresser, sir," Hicks said, producing a towel.

Jason waited impatiently while his brother washed.

"What is this harsh treatment poor Miss Groton has endured?" Jason finally asked, after his frustration rose to the level of hunting for worms to fish in the river as a lad.

"Her father was a shopkeeper in Oxford, but when he died, she had no one to turn to. When the business was foreclosed, she found herself out on the street." Charlie tossed down the towel and disappeared again as Hicks threw a fresh linen shirt over his head. "She didn't have so much as a groat in her pocket and had to make her way to her Aunt Bessie in Cheapside, so Basil promised she could spend the night in his digs then get the stage the next day. But it didn't turn out that way, as you know."

"It's about the only thing I do know," Jason said.

"There's a chap who runs a gambling house in Oxford. He's the devil's spawn! Has an interest in a club here in London as well. He's demanding Miss Groton pay her father's gambling debts. She hasn't the ready to pay him. The fellow's a sharper, Jas."

"That's the extent of it?"

"Not entirely." Charlie slipped on the gold waistcoat Hicks held out to him. "He's here in London at his club. If she can't meet Pomfret's demands, he'll have her work for him until it's paid off."

"I gather it's not as a maid?"

"No. That's just it." Charlie cleared his throat. "She's

quite pretty. And sweet, Jas, as you'll see."

Jason already saw a lot. He rose from the chair and moved it back against the wall. He had formed the deep suspicion that this young lady was not what Charlie believed she was. Still, he didn't like to see her held to ransom by crooks, if what she said was true. He would certainly need to be on his toes tonight. "I'll see you in the drawing room in an hour. Don't be late."

"But you haven't said if —"

Jason held up his hand as he stalked out the door.

CHAPTER FIVE

In the small attic room, Helen stood with Diana and Toby around Bart's bed. His arm lay by his side over the coverlet, his face deeply etched with pain. She patted the footman's hand. Pink scalp showed through his once thick brown hair.

Bart groaned. He opened his eyes but didn't seem to see her. "Tell Captain Peyton, I'm sorry."

Shocked, Helen clasped his hand tighter. "What about Lord Peyton, Bart?"

"Couldn't help. Thought it best… couldn't tell your mother…" Bart's unfocussed gaze found her face. "Be careful, Lady Helen, you must find out…" His voice a bare whisper, he closed his eyes.

"I will, Bart. I promise." Tears flooded her vision. She had no idea what he wanted her to discover, but he had slipped away from her. Was he warning her, or had he been muddled with sickness and pain?

"He's heavily drugged with an opiate and has not long now. He won't say anything more, poor fellow," said the surgeon, a quietly spoken man of some fifty years. "You must leave." He spread his arms to encompass them and guided them from the room.

"What would Bart have kept from Mama?" Toby asked, his voice wobbling with distress. "And why was he sorry about Lord Peyton?"

"We must ask him," Diana said, her voice muffled by her handkerchief.

Helen silently agreed. Had her earlier suspicions of Lord Peyton been rooted in fact? "We must tell Mama what Bart said." They descended the servants' stairs from the attic. "And Papa will know what to do when he returns."

"I wish he was here," Toby said.

Diana sniffed. "Shall we have to wear mourning clothes and cancel my ball?"

"No, dearest. Bart's not a relative." Helen put an arm around her sister's waist. This was a terrible shock to them all, but perhaps it affected Diana more than her. Toby, although upset, considered himself a man. Despite Diana's self-confidence, she was young and had never seen a death at close quarters. Even though Helen had witnessed their Aunt Violet's laying out, she still shivered with shock.

"How very strange," Mama said on learning of Bart's last words. "I shall notify Lord Peyton. And I must write to Bartholomew's mother. I believe she lives in a village in Cumbria and is unlikely to travel all the way to London for the funeral.

"Now my dears, the surgeon wishes to see me." After

kissing them both, Mama extricated herself from the morning room sofa, where Helen and Diana had huddled beside her. She put a hand on Toby's shoulder where he slumped in a chair. "Do not be too distressed. Bartholomew is no longer in pain. God cares for him in heaven."

Helen watched her mother leave the room. How very curious it was. Lord Peyton must have waited at the foot of their garden with the intention of meeting Bart. And he'd inveigled himself into their house on what now seemed to be a ruse. Her breath hitched. She rubbed Diana's arm as she leaned against her. They'd all been drawn to Peyton's appealing, amusing manner. And thought him kind to promise to introduce Toby to Mr. Nash. He'd appeared so trustworthy. Was that a ruse too? How could she believe anything he now said? She hoped her mother would discover what lay behind this awful business, but if she didn't, Helen was determined to.

~~~

Dark-haired Baron Bianchi was of average height, with those liquid deep brown eyes that displayed a surfeit of emotion, almost at will. Fortunately, there was little in his mode of dress for Jason to suspect him to be one of those Latins he detested, who wooed a lady with flattery then revealed themselves to be corrupt at the core. Bianchi's midnight blue tailcoat and white embroidered waistcoat were unremarkable, his only affectation a large emerald of a superior quality on the ring finger of his right hand. Jason imagined women would find him attractive. His sister undoubtedly did.

The baron accepted a glass of wine from the footman, and they seated themselves in the drawing room.

"How do you find our weather, Baron?"

"Forgive me for saying so, but it rains rather often," he said with an apologetic shrug. "And the sun, it is not as warm here as in Italy. Have you visited my country, my lord?"

"Yes. A brief stay." Jason was not about to elaborate. He had accompanied the Foreign Secretary, Viscount Castlereagh, to Italy during the Congress of Vienna, when Napoleon returned to France during the hundred days after his escape from Elba. Jason then fought under Wellington at the Battle of Waterloo. Fortunately, Bianchi knew better than to ask.

"As you would be aware, Napoleon's family hailed from Italy before they went to Corsica. Italian was the general's first language." Bianchi raised a black eyebrow with quizzical amusement. "I feel I must apologize for the appalling actions of my countryman."

"Please don't think I will hold it against you." Jason smiled as the door opened and Lizzie entered.

He and Bianchi stood as his sister, dressed in a surprisingly frivolous deep lavender silk gown, the skirts and sleeves a mass of ruffles, came to take Bianchi's hand.

"How very glad I am you could come on such short notice, Baron Bianchi."

"I would have braved a snowstorm to be here, tonight,

Lady Greywood," Bianchi replied in his heavily accented voice, his gaze capturing hers for a long moment.

"Thankfully, that wasn't necessary," Jason said, pouring a little cold water on the heated atmosphere. He met Lizzie's fiery glance and smiled. "Just a little rain, Baron, of which we English are quite accustomed."

"Ah, yes, rain." The baron nodded sympathetically.

Charlie entered with Russell, who announced two ladies. Although Charlie had said Amelia Groton was pretty, Jason had not expected such a beauty. The slender young woman in pale pink was a perfect English rose with creamy skin, wheat-gold hair drawn into a topknot to display a graceful neck, and eyes the blue of an English summer sky. Her Aunt Bessie, tightly corseted in purple, cast a nervous glance around the room while clutching a rope of jet beads at her breast.

Charlie drew them both forward. "Allow me to introduce my sister, Lady Greywood, and my brother, Captain, Lord Peyton. Lizzie, Jas, please meet Mrs. Groton and her niece, Miss Groton. And this must be Baron Bianchi. How do you do."

Jason watched as Amelia's speculative blue gaze roamed the drawing room from the swags of silk damask at the windows to the elegant furniture, the white columns decorating brick red walls hung with fine art and mirrors. She revealed none of her aunt's nervousness when she turned to Jason. With a demure smile, she offered him her gloved fingers.

"So very kind of you to invite us, my lord."

"My pleasure, Miss Groton." Jason raised her small hand to his lips.

As the rest of the introductions followed, Jason grew increasingly uneasy. If Charlie had a yen to make Miss Amelia Groton his wife, and many red-blooded men would be tempted, it would be very difficult to dissuade him.

Jason had Miss Groton's measure at first glance. While he was sympathetic to any young woman unprotected and at the mercy of some scoundrel, she would not marry Charlie.

Bianchi, however, was not so easy to read. Some digging was required into the gentleman's circumstances. Jason had a friend residing in Florence. He would write to him tonight.

In the dining room, as Russell supervised the footmen bringing in the first course, Jason turned to the baron on his left, acutely aware of Lizzie listening to their conversation from across the table. "What has brought you to London, Baron?"

"I have made fine art my interest, my lord. I particularly like the da Vinci drawing of a horse on that far wall. I suppose you don't wish to sell it? No? I should not like to part with it myself," he said when Jason shook his head. "I am presenting an exhibition of Renaissance art here in London, at a Mayfair gallery. Some of the works are from my estate in Florence, a Titian amongst them. Perhaps you'd care to attend the opening? It is on Thursday."

"Thank you. Regretfully, I have another engagement on Thursday."

"A pity. The exhibition will run for the following two weeks."

"Then I look forward to seeing it." He smiled at Lizzie, who toyed with her spoon. "You will accompany me, won't you, Lizzie?"

She smiled gratefully at him. "Such works of art require more than one viewing."

Miss Groton was giggling flirtatiously at something Charlie had said. His brother's flushed face betrayed his fascination as Mrs. Groton looked on with a fond expression.

Jason groaned inwardly.

The evening passed without incident. When the front door closed on their guests, Lizzie paused at the foot of the stairs before retiring.

Something was required of him. "The baron has a great deal of charm, Lizzie," Jason said as they made their way upstairs. After dinner, over port, Bianchi had spoken effusively of his ancient villa and gardens, which he hoped Jason and Lizzie would visit one day. "I am keen to view what promises to be a superb collection."

"There is more to him than charm and his artworks, Jas," she said, sounding exasperated.

"You've only just met the baron, my dear. But by all means, take the time to get to know him."

With an affectionate smile, she took his arm. "Do you fear that if we should marry he'll whisk me off to Italy?"

That seemed so final it chilled him. Lizzie at her new husband's mercy in some foreign country didn't bear thinking about. Had he become too protective? He was determined not to let his own desire to keep her close and safe motivate him. "Of course, I would miss you. Very much. But it's early days, Lizzie."

Reaching her door, he turned to her. "Apart from the fellow's obvious good looks, what is it about him that so captivates you?"

She paused for a moment, one hand on the doorknob. Her eyes were sad when she looked at him. "His warmth, I suppose. I adored Greywood, as you know. I wanted to die after he was shot. But he was brutalized by his years away at war. It was not always easy to get as close as I would have liked."

She was right of course. Jason bowed his head in agreement. The war changed men. A captain in the Foot Guards, Robert Greywood had lost most of his men at the advance of the French cavalry and artillery. He only talked about it when he and Jason had imbibed a good deal of brandy. And Jason knew Robert would never speak of it to Lizzie. The horror of battle was etched forever in his and Jason's soul. How Greywood described wave upon wave of the French cuirassiers advancing, shouting, *"Vive l'Empereur."* How his men had knelt, their bayonets raised, like a line of impassable steel, to thwart them. And then to watch so many of them fall. A man doesn't forget that.

"I only ask you to take your time, Lizzie. Don't be swept off your feet." He kissed her cheek and continued along the passage.

In his sitting room, Charlie sprawled in a chair. "Well,

what do you think of Amelia, Jas?"

Jason buried a sigh. He longed for a few moments of uncomplicated peace, and he had that letter to write. "I thought her exceedingly pretty."

"She's a beauty. Sweet natured too." Charlie jumped up and followed Jason into his dressing room, where Hicks waited. "You will help her, won't you, Jas?"

"I promise I'll try. But I refuse to discuss it now while I undress. As charming as Miss Groton is, she does not equal my need for sleep."

Charlie chuckled and slapped him on the back. "It's barely one o'clock. Shall I begin to call you 'old fellow'?"

"Only if you desire to be sent to Coventry," Jason said with a grin.

An idea had come to him. The best way to deal with Miss Groton was to solve her immediate problem and banish the scoundrel who threatened her. Once she no longer required Charlie's help, a young man such as he, with no means to support her for years, would fade into the background while London discovered a new beauty in their midst. As far as Jason could tell, although Charlie was captivated, he had not fallen deeply in love with Amelia Groton. Not yet at least.

Late the next morning, Jason woke to the sound of church bells ringing out over London. Russell delivered a note with his morning coffee.

"This just came, my lord. I thought it prudent to bring it to you immediately."

Jason stretched and yawned. "Can't a fellow have some

peace on a Sunday? Thank you, Russell, you are, as always, correct to have done so." He examined the letter and, as the butler withdrew, opened it.

I apologize for disturbing you on the Sabbath, my lord, but an urgent matter has arisen. I consider it imprudent to wait for my husband to return or to put the reason for this missive in writing. I wonder if you could visit me this afternoon? I would be most grateful.

The note was signed Grace Kinsey.

Jason tossed the blankets back and leaped from the bed, more than a little intrigued and hopeful that he might be about to learn what lay behind this mysterious so-called wild-goose chase Parnell had sent him on. With any luck, he could report back to Parnell and put the whole damned business behind him by the end of the week. Then he could concentrate on other pressing matters, like sorting out Miss Groton's problem and delve, albeit subtly, into the baron's past. He needed to discover if the man was decent, for Lizzie's sake, before their relationship deepened.

After washing and dressing, he made his way downstairs. In the breakfast room, as he scooped ham and eggs onto his plate from the heated dishes on the sideboard, he was hit by an unpleasant thought. What if his findings did crush Charlie's and Lizzie's plans for their futures? He would become persona non grata in his own house. It would require him removing himself to Peyton Grove, a place he usually found appealing, but just now, the prospect of returning alone to his country seat was not so captivating. Self-examination was not something Jason normally indulged in. He wasn't sure why he'd begun to question his life, but he refused to give the credit to Parnell.

CHAPTER SIX

A black armband on his sleeve, Fiske opened the door to Jason. "Lady Kinsey will see you in the library, my lord. Please follow me?"

Jason crossed the expanse of exotic Eastern carpet as Lady Kinsey rose from a maroon leather chesterfield to greet him.

Kinsey's library was an assault on the senses, crammed with relics from his travels. Stone effigies perched on tables and in glass-fronted cabinets. On the walls shelf upon shelf was filled with aged leather-bound tomes and interesting Egyptian, Greek, and Roman artifacts Jason would like more time to examine. The dry, dusty smell of antiquity was foreign and inimitable. By the window, a broad walnut desk was neatly stacked with papers and books. Against one wall in a corner of the room an alarming, gigantic sarcophagus stood upright, belonging to some long dead Egyptian. Jason wondered briefly how Kinsey came by the coffin and if it should be in a museum. He turned to greet his hostess.

"Unnerving, isn't it? Kinsey was intrigued to find one so

roomy, with a cleverly hinged door. He wondered if it might have been meant for a couple. The mummy, or mummies, have been removed, thank goodness. He only has it on loan. Thank you for responding so promptly, Lord Peyton."

"I am pleased to be of service, my lady."

He'd thought Lady Kinsey a self-assured woman when he first met her, but it appeared her cool reserve had been shattered. Her gray eyes were dark and anxious, her hands constantly in motion as she urged him to be seated and settled her garnet-colored skirts around her.

"I thought it best to receive you here in the library where we are unlikely to be disturbed. I don't want my children involved." She placed her nervous hands together in her lap. "Now, perhaps you could enlighten me as to why our footman, now deceased, wished to apologize to you, almost with his dying breath."

"Your footman, my lady? I have no idea." Jason fought for time to order his thoughts. It was clear that their footman was his contact who had failed to meet him because of illness, and Lady Kinsey, no fool by the look of it, eyed him suspiciously.

"You said you worked for Mr. Nash. Is that true?"

"Why do you doubt it, my lady?"

"The doctor has informed me that my footman was poisoned, Lord Peyton. Systematically. So, as you see, I am determined to get to the bottom of something that obviously involved you in some fashion."

Jason's blood went cold. "I wish I could offer an

explanation. Set you at your ease, at least. But at this moment, I can tell you nothing. As far as I know, I have never met your footman."

"Then why did Bartholomew Smyth say to my daughter, Helen, 'tell Captain Peyton I am sorry'?"

Jason sat forward. "Bartholomew Smyth was your footman? He fought alongside me in Belgium!" He sighed. "Bart's dead?"

"Yes, poor man."

An explanation was clearly called for. Jason picked his words carefully. "I do not work for Mr. Nash. But I was acting on his behalf, to perform a duty that he or one of his staff would have done by explaining those changes that we have discussed. I must confess to a more important reason. An acquaintance of mine, a government official, recently contacted me about an unsigned letter they'd received. Someone wished to speak to me personally on a matter of significant importance. As the letter writer did not furnish their name or address, beyond working in one of the houses along the Queen's Walk, I had no idea who it was or where to find him. He was to approach me at a certain time in that area of the park that faces your property. I'm sorry I could not explain this before, Lady Kinsey, but I had no way of knowing if it was your house I sought. But rest assured I have every intention of looking into it."

He raked his hair with his fingers. "I wish I'd known it was Bartholomew. He fought bravely and was invalided out of the army after he lost an arm." Jason shook his head. "I fear this mystery might have died with him.

"Bow Street has been advised?"

"A constable from the Magistrate's Court called yesterday. He said Bart's death was likely due to accidental poisoning and saw no reason to draw the magistrate's attention to it."

"I'd like to speak to the doctor."

"Yes, of course. Do whatever you feel is right."

"May I see your footman's room?"

"His effects have been removed."

"Nevertheless, I feel it wise."

"Very well." She rose from the sofa. "Better perhaps if I accompany you."

As they made their way along the corridor toward the rear of the building and the servants' stairs, Lady Helen appeared from one of the reception rooms, wearing an apron over her gray dress.

Jason eyed her appreciatively as she put a hand to her abundant chestnut locks, becomingly tied up with a green ribbon. She looked upon him with some measure of distrust. He couldn't blame her. He'd disliked the subterfuge and now had to find a way to repair it.

"Good afternoon, Lord Peyton. I wasn't aware we had a visitor." She whisked off the apron and smoothed down her skirts.

Jason bowed. "Lady Helen."

"Helen, where are Diana and Toby?"

"In the garden playing shuttlecock, Mama."

"Good. Lord Peyton and I are about to inspect

Bartholomew's room."

Helen widened tip-tilted gray eyes very much like her mother's. "Why, Mama? Have you learned something more?"

Lady Kinsey explained Jason's connection to Bart while Lady Helen's eyes continued to coolly assess him. Lady Kinsey placed a hand on her daughter's arm. "You had best come too, Helen. You've had more to do with Bartholomew. Diana and Toby are not to learn of this."

"You cannot speak of this to anyone, Lady Helen," Jason warned. He considered her being drawn into this was ill judged, but her mother had obviously come to entrust her with matters that should be dealt with by someone far older. He found himself intrigued enough to want to discover more about Lady Helen. She was like a calm millpond, but he sensed a strong current flowing beneath the surface. And she was frowning at him.

She glanced at her mother and then gave a nod of consent. "I understand."

The kitchen noises and aromas reached them as they climbed the narrow wooden servants' staircase to the attics. Lady Helen gathered up her skirts to follow in her mother's wake.

Jason observed the young lady's neat ankles, her narrow back, and the pleasing curve of her hip revealed by the taut fabric while he trailed behind her. Again, he wondered why she was not yet married. Might she be engaged? He had not heard of it. But then that wasn't surprising since he didn't read the society gossip columns in the newspapers and he seldom attended balls or soirées. He glanced at her hand on the banister. No ring. That was not conclusive, but somehow, he knew he was right. It would take a determined man to break through that wall of reserve and suspicion, and he was patently aware that, in this instance, he was the cause of it.

Jason looked away from a glossy chestnut curl resting on her delicate nape, which seemed somehow vulnerable and intimate and at odds with her stoic, standoffish manner. His interest surprised him. He wasn't in the business of seeking a bride. There was no urgency to produce an heir. If he failed, Charlie would become earl after him. And even if Lizzie didn't marry the baron, she would remarry and produce appealing offspring. Apart from that pleasant avuncular role, no one would make any claim on him.

Bart's attic room was as he'd expected, simply furnished with an iron bed beneath the sloping roof. Evidence of his efforts to make it homelier were in the cheerful picture of a dog on the wall and a bright rug covering the boards. A comfortable chair sat in one corner. The mattress had been stripped and the bedding folded. On the table were a candlestick, matches, and, incongruously, several blank sheets of superior quality vellum, an inkpot, blotter, and a pen. The door to the small empty cupboard stood open.

"Bartholomew's effects have been returned to his family," Lady Kinsey said.

"A pity. Was it only his clothes?"

"I don't know what was sent. My housekeeper, Mrs.

Chance, saw to it."

"I shall need to speak to her."

Jason pulled open the curtains. A dismal ray of sunlight crept in beneath the eaves to fall upon the floor. He lifted the mattress and found nothing beneath it then knelt and peered under the bed. Straightening, he went to the small fireplace.

"The housemaids have yet to clean the room," Lady Kinsey said.

Jason stirred the embers in the grate with the iron poker. He leaned in and picked up a wedge of paper, burned around the edges. The same quality bond as those on the table, written on in an untidy manner, badly smeared, and scorched by the fire. "I gather Bart could read and write."

"Yes. His grandmother taught him when he was a boy. He wished to better himself and was hoping to find clerical work," Lady Helen said with a catch in her voice. "He managed very well with one arm. I've been helping him to write to various businesses."

He held the paper out to her. "Do you think this might have been such a letter?"

As she took it, her fingers brushed against his. A feather-light touch and yet, he was very much aware of it. She was, too, he guessed because her cheeks colored up and she stepped away.

She studied the fragment in her hands. "This isn't anything we worked on together." She looked skeptical. "Surely it isn't of importance? The words are mostly indecipherable."

"We shouldn't dismiss it out of hand." He resisted

taking it from her, watching as she lowered her head over it again.

"This word could be 'threat' or 'thread.'" She gazed up at him, her eyebrows drawing closer, clearly wondering why he bothered to examine it. "The rest of that line is too badly smudged to make out." She held it out to him.

He shook his head. "You're doing well. Please continue."

She looked again at the fragment. "Could this be 'truth'? But two words on the lower line are most odd, 'electric fish'? Her gaze darted to his. "Might Bart refer to an electric eel? I've heard of those in South America. Although why...?" She shook her head. "It cannot be of interest surely." She handed the fragment back to him.

"One does not delve into a servant's personal life," Lady Kinsey said, obviously losing patience. "They are entitled to their privacy as much as we are."

"Jeremy, our other footman, might be able to help," Lady Helen said, paying her mother no heed. "Or Eloise, Mama's French maid. Bart enjoyed their conversations in her language. He had picked up a smattering of French during his time on the Continent."

He almost smiled at her sudden reluctance to drop the matter.

"I'll speak to them after I've seen the doctor." Jason crouched down to rake the ashes. "There's nothing more here." He straightened. "This letter was destroyed for a reason. I find that surprising. Why would Bart waste good vellum by writing something he did not intend to post? That's expensive paper for a footman to have. I assume you supplied it, Lady Helen?"

She flushed and darted a look at her mother. "Yes."

At Lady Kinsey's expression, Jason suspected more would be said on the matter, once he'd left them.

"I'll examine this more closely." He took out his wallet and placed the paper carefully inside before tucking it back into his pocket.

They returned downstairs. "Thank you for coming, my lord," Lady Kinsey said after furnishing him with the surgeon's address. "Please keep me advised about anything you might discover."

"Rest assured I shall make every effort to learn what happened to your footman, my lady. And try to find out what prompted Bart to seek my help."

"It's distressing to think of how much he suffered," Lady Helen said sadly as they made their way along the corridor.

Fiske had just admitted a gentleman through the front door.

Lady Kinsey greeted him. "Lord Peyton, may I introduce Mr. Thorburn to you. Mr. Thorburn is Kinsey's secretary. I would be grateful if you would address any concerns you have concerning Bartholomew to this gentleman."

Fair-haired, Thorburn was somewhere in his mid to late thirties with the pasty complexion of those who spent most of their lives indoors at a desk. Behind his wire-framed spectacles, his hazel eyes were keen and alert. He bowed with a polite smile. "Certainly, my lord. A dreadful business to be sure. If I may make a comment?"

Jason nodded. "Please do."

"It is my belief that the medicine Bart took daily could have been poisonous. He did tell me he was interested in improving his diet with the use of an herbal libation. Suffered some digestion troubles, if you'll pardon me mentioning the indelicate subject, Lady Kinsey. Told me he purchased the tonic at a shop in Whitechapel."

Jason frowned. "Where is the bottle?"

"I gave it to the doctor, my lord," Fiske said.

Lady Kinsey turned to him. "Fiske? You knew about this?"

"Yes, my lady. Bartholomew showed me the tonic. I advised him not to take the evil-smelling liquid."

Thorburn excused himself, citing much to be done before Lord Kinsey returned.

Jason pondered this information as he took his hat, gloves, and brass-topped cane from the butler. "Please send word if you have need of me before Lord Kinsey returns. Good day, Lady Kinsey, Lady Helen."

When Jason paused in the street to pull on his gloves, the front door opened and Lady Helen hurried after him down the path. Her worried eyes searched his. "Mother forgot to mention Jinx. He's our kitchen boy. Jinx fell sick at the same time as Bart, but has since recovered."

He wished he could reassure her. But he feared matters

were likely to get worse. "It is something to investigate. Thank you for telling me. "

Her eyes narrowed slightly. "Do you have any idea why Bart would have asked for you most particularly?"

He huffed out a sigh at her obvious distrust of him. "Apart from my being his captain during the war? I'm afraid I don't."

She tilted her head. "Strange, though, don't you think, after all this time?"

Was she interrogating him? "It would seem so. At least until we find the answer. If you can't think of anything else?" He half turned toward the road.

"Bart had become quite nervous recently," she said, delaying him once again. "He'd grown careless in his appearance, which upset Fiske, and he had cross words with Mrs. Chance. It was unlike him. He didn't confide in me. But I will see if I can find out something more."

He cursed under his breath. "That's not wise, Lady Helen. Leave this to me. Please exercise care until this matter is resolved."

She put a hand to the curls at her temple. "How does one exercise care in one's own home?"

He paused. "This matter may have little to do with the inhabitants of Kinsey House." He wished the reason for Bart's horrible death could be easily explained. "You might consider retiring to the country with your siblings for a time if you are concerned."

"I have no intention of leaving London, my lord."

"Until your father returns?"

"No. Diana's ball is soon to be held. She certainly won't go to the country, and neither will I." Her dark lashes swept down, a habit he'd noticed she adopted when she wished to hide her feelings. "I'll ask Mama if she'll send the boys to our grandfather. Toby loves to visit Walcott. There's so much more for him to do there. He can ride with the hounds and fish in the river. But Alexander, he's only a baby and will kick up a fuss if I don't go." She surprised him with the first unequivocal look she'd afforded him. "I was wool gathering. I do apologize, my lord. This can be of no interest to you. We are all so distressed about Bart."

He smiled, taking in her delicate features as wisps of chestnut hair stirred in the breeze exposing a crescent-shaped scar near her ear. "Perfectly understandable. And remember, not a word to anyone. Good day, Lady Helen."

She hesitated. "I should like you to keep me informed. With my father away, and Mama busy with her latest charity, it behooves me to deal with these matters."

"Of course." He was pleased he hadn't revealed his shock at that statement. How did she think of herself, twenty-four going on forty? He watched her walk briskly away down the path. And she was wrong. Everything about the Kinsey family was now of intense interest to him. Jason walked along the street. He'd always managed a pleasant rapport with his servants, but the Kinseys seemed to care a great deal for their staff. He suspected that Lady Helen was, by nature, a mother hen. Had she decided to trust him? Or was she still reserving her opinion? She would not trust easily, he suspected.

It could be that Bart ingested arsenic or even mercury in some tonic he bought. Systematic poisoning pointed to regular doses, either by him or administered by someone else. It wasn't an accident. The footman had something important to tell him. It was too convenient for him to be silenced so neatly. If only Bart had added his name and address to the letter, Jason might have been able to save him. The possibility brought him to a stop, and he curled his fingers around the green-painted wrought iron fence enclosing the entry and stairs leading to the basement of a townhouse and stared blankly, forcing his thoughts back to the war.

Some of his army friends liked to relive the glory of battle when they gathered together in some tavern. Jason did not. He left it to his dreams. But Bart's death brought it back in all its gory horror.

It had rained during that night of the last campaign. While he stood here in Mayfair, he could almost detect the metallic smell of blood, mingling with the malodourous odors of farm animals and mud, the heavy moisture-laden air thick enough to choke a man. The screams and groans of the injured men and horses that rent the air came back with startling clarity.

After the British, under Colonel MacDonnell, had taken over the range of chateau buildings at Hougoumont, Jason spent the night working with the men, building fire steps and loopholing, which made narrow slits in the walls. All the gates were blocked, other than the main gate on the northern side to provide access.

On the morning of the eighteenth of June, the French
attacked the chateau. They surged around the buildings and
charged the main gate. Under the barrage, the gate was
damaged. It became a deathly struggle to keep the French
from swarming inside. Finally, Jason and a party of British
and German soldiers were able to force the gate shut, and
Sergeant Graham of the Coldstream Guards put the bar in
place. After it was fortified, Jason led a group of men to hunt
down the few French soldiers who had slipped through and
roamed the outbuildings.

The attack on the château continued hour after hour,
and during the afternoon, the supply of ammunition began
to dwindle. Corporal Bartholomew Smyth volunteered to
drive the ammunition wagon through the French lines. The
young man argued forcefully that his childhood spent in
Cumbria, the wettest county in England, lent him the
advantage of being able to drive fast over the muddy
ground. Jason had watched him go off toward the main line
with little hope the lad would return. Two hours later, a
cheer went up, when Bart, bleeding heavily from a nasty
wound to his arm, arrived with a wagon of cartridges.

They held on when Napoleon ordered the château be
razed to the ground. Howitzer shells demolished the château
and set it ablaze. In the final closing hours of the battle,
despite heavy casualties, and only the chapel left standing,
they prevailed. The French failed to capture Hougoumont,
and the woods and fields around it were strewn with their

dead and dying.

Later, Jason visited Bart, whose wound was being tended to. He poured a considerable amount of his whiskey down the young corporal's throat from his flask before the sawbones sawed off Bart's arm at the elbow. Jason had seen many acts of valor during the war, but Bart's cheeky young face, good humor, and stunning bravery remained in his memory.

Jason was only too aware that thousands of ex-soldiers like Bart flooded into London after the war. Jason had employed a few himself, sending some to his country estate. The small government pension did little to help them overcome their injuries, find work, or deal with the changed circumstances they'd returned to. It had disgusted Jason and caused him to lose heart. That Bart had been taken back into the Kinsey household as footman, even though he'd lost an arm, said a good deal about them.

With a soft curse, Jason pushed away from the railings and continued along the street, vowing to find Bart's murderer.

He raised his cane to a passing hackney.

"Whitehall, if you please, jarvey," he ordered, climbing inside.

"Right you are, guv."

As the carriage turned into Pall Mall, Jason thought again of the compassionate Lady Helen. Most young women were more concerned with finding a suitable man to marry than taking care of staff. Bart must have appreciated her kindness.

He removed the fragment from his wallet but, even in broad daylight, still could not make out the blurred words. He put it away again as the jarvey pulled the carriage to a stop.

~~~

Helen entered the morning room, feeling uneasy about Lord Peyton. Why was she drawn to confide in him? To trust him when she knew so little about him? It was unlike her to allow his good looks and manliness to affect her judgment. And it would be foolish to put her trust in him before she found out what lay behind his involvement. Bart deserved her objectivity. She had promised him she would find out the truth.

"Where have you been?" Diana asked. "I wanted to show you the riding hat featured in this month's *La Belle Assemblée*." She held the page up, showing a hat of a rather flamboyant design.

"I was just seeing Lord Peyton out. I don't care for it. You'd have enough feathers to fly with."

"Peyton was here?" Diana frowned. "And you didn't tell me?"

Helen did not like keeping secrets from her sister but knew she must shield her from this worry. "I wasn't aware of it myself until I came across him in the passage with Mama. He didn't stay long. He wasn't here on a social visit."

Diana turned the page of her magazine. "Was it concerning Bart?"

"Yes. Peyton was his captain during the war."

"Oh, really? How remarkable. What did Peyton have to say?"

"He is trying to find out why Bart wished to see him."

The confusing mystery nagged at her. Had someone threatened Bart or even deliberately harmed him? What did those strange words written on the burned fragment mean? Would Peyton be able to make out more of it and discover their significance? If he did, would he tell her? Infuriating how women were shielded as if they were fragile ornaments to be tucked away somewhere safe. Even he had suggested she leave London. It was all she could do not to snap at him, when he really didn't deserve it. He was obviously trying to protect them. She bit her lip. There she was making excuses for him. He was a man after all. And some men could be underhanded and ruthless. Well, she would continue to investigate on her own. She might find something of interest to aid him. Warming to the plan, she hoped another chance would come to talk with him and learn his thoughts. Something incomprehensible had occurred when their hands had touched. She still wondered at it. She must be on her guard and not be taken in by his clear green eyes, which appeared so compelling and trustworthy. Or his deep voice, which carried such authority. Bart had put his trust in him. But Bart was dead.

"Helen?"

Helen looked up from toying with the scalloped edge of her sleeve. "Mm?"

"I just asked if Peyton plans to call again."

"Yes. When Papa arrives home."

"Oh, that's good. I'll be sure to see him."

"You can hardly lurk in the corridor or force your way into the library. Papa would be cross."

"Papa is never cross for long." Diana giggled. "Mama and I are to visit the dressmaker tomorrow for the final fitting of my ball gown. I can't wait for you to see it. Mama insisted I wear white because all debutantes do, but I did want something that would make me stand out. It is lovely though. I'm sure you'll agree."

"You will stand out, dearest," Helen said confidently. "You'd look lovely if you were dressed in a jute sack."

Diana laughed. "Well, it's certainly not a sack. Do you think if I asked Papa to invite Lord Peyton to my ball, he would come, and dance with me?"

"He might. You can only ask." Helen bit her lip at the flood of intense jealousy that snaked through her. She was still trying to reason with herself when their mother entered the room.

"Here you are. I have decided your idea is an excellent one, Helen. Toby and Alexander are to stay with your grandfather for a few weeks. And Miss Prince is to accompany them."

"Toby will like that. He is dreadfully fatiguing when he has nothing to occupy his time, but why are you sending Alexander?" Diana glanced at Helen. "He won't want to go without Helen."

"Nonsense," Mama said. "There is still much to be done

to prepare for the ball. Alexander loves Miss Prince, and your grandfather spoils him most dreadfully. They will leave for Walcott tomorrow."

"I might go with them and help Miss Prince settle Alexander in," Helen suggested.

"But you might miss my ball!" Diana cried.

"Diana is quite correct. If we have a spate of bad weather, the roads could become impassable." A small smile tugged Mama's lips as she walked to the door. "You must wear your new gown. It cost your father a small fortune." She paused a hand on the doorknob. "I need to discuss a matter with Mrs. Chance. Come and see me in my sitting room in fifteen minutes, please, Helen."

Was she in trouble? As the door closed behind their mother, Helen traced the scar at her temple, unnerved. Nothing would sway Mama when she was determined. Didn't Papa always say so?

She had not wished for a new dress. She loathed balls, and anyway, it was Diana's night to shine.

Helen had not enjoyed a social occasion for years. Not since she danced twice with a handsome gentleman and strolled in the perfumed garden by moonlight. He had proved himself not to be a gentleman at all, as it turned out. Instead, he was a cold, unfeeling rake.

"My goodness, your face! What ghastly thing are you thinking about?" Diana asked.

Diana had never been told the extent of Helen's fall from grace, and Helen wasn't about to tell her now. "That I shall have men crushing my toes again," she said, "and either treating me with indifference or sympathy."

Diana shook her head. "You never know, you might meet the man of your dreams."

Peyton's lean face appeared in her mind's eye, and annoyed with herself, she feared she already had.

In answer to her mother's summons, Helen found her at the small desk in her sitting room, the household accounts open before her. One finger absently toyed with a curl at her neck.

"May I help you with the accounts, Mama?" Helen asked, pleased to find something to distract her mother from her purpose.

"No thank you." Mama pushed back her chair, rose, then sat on the small tapestry sofa, gesturing for Helen to join her.

Helen sat, bracing herself for one of Mama's talks.

"You must not give up on life, dear child."

Helen sighed. "I haven't Mama."

"If not marriage, what do you plan for your future?"

"Harry insists he will never marry. I thought I might live with him at Cherrywood, when the time comes, and assist him in managing the estate. I am rather good at that sort of thing."

Mama put an arm around her. "My dear child. Your brother might state at the ripe old age of twenty-two that he has no wish to marry, but I assure you he *will* change his mind."

"Not everyone marries, Mama."

"No. Not everyone is suited to it. But you are. You're practical and capable. You are also very loving. Surely you want to be a mother one day?"

"I don't expect to." That was unfair. A pain struck deep in Helen's ribs, and she drew in a slow breath. "I don't know how you can say…"

Mama patted her hand. "Because I know that life moves on and brings with it change. Be brave, my dear. Now go along. I have much to do."

Helen made her way downstairs. Was she cowardly? She'd considered her decision to be an honorable one. She ran her hand down the smooth wooden banister, her plan still solidly in place. Once Diana married, Helen would refuse to come to London for another Season. She would remain at Cherrywood. She continued down with a sigh. To be there again in June when the wild roses and blackberry were in bloom and the pretty house martins with their short, feathered legs collected mud for their nests. To sit by the pond and watch the demoiselle dragonflies skim across the water. It was a balm to her wounded soul. She could be content there. The ancient house set in its lovely park required a keen hand to run it, even before it became Harry's, and Mama with her charities and Papa with his explorations showed little interest.

CHAPTER SEVEN

At the sound of a trumpet, Jason looked out Parnell's office window and was caught by the colorful display made by the mounted King's Life Guard in their red tunics and white-plumed helmets and the Blues and Royals in their blue tunics and red-plumed helmets. Mounted on their immaculately groomed horses with breastplates shining in the sun, they assembled on the north side of the Horse Guards enclosure.

Parnell leaned back in his chair and formed a steeple with his fingers. "We still have the problem of this threat to the country's security. We can leave the murder of the footman for Bow Street to deal with. The government cannot be seen to spend more time and waste resources on what might be the fanciful notions of a footman now deceased, but it appears that we must get to the bottom of Smythe's letter in case there is any substance to the threat.

"I find it impossible to suspect Lord Kinsey of being involved. Smythe may have heard about the threat elsewhere."

"I'd be happy to continue with the investigation, but outside of Kinsey House, I have nothing to go on." Jason flicked a gaze at Parnell's shrewd eyes. He saw no reason to explain that he owed it to Bart. Parnell was a hardnosed member of the War Office, where everyone was seen to be expendable for the right cause and, sometimes, the wrong one. He must always have his eye to the bigger picture, the security and protection of England.

"Then continue on." The spymaster cocked an eyebrow. "No woman involved in this who you feel you should rescue is there?"

Jason tightened his jaw, as the heavy weight of responsibility settled over his shoulders. "Yes, several, as a matter of fact, and two young males. Lord Kinsey is away in the East."

Parnell gave him a wry glance then picked up a sheath of papers. "Send Bartlett in on your way out. And keep me informed."

Leaving Whitehall, Jason made his way to Mr. Belvedere's home in Curzon Street. A solidly built man in his fifties, he was a member of the Royal College of Surgeons, who Jason considered to be a cut above the self-serving quacks and sawbones he'd dealt with in the past.

Belvedere pushed the tonic bottle across the desk to Jason. "I've tested this. Arsenic. There was enough to prostrate Smyth while slowly killing him. I might have suspected poisoning, but other symptoms masked it. The patient had not told me he was taking a tonic. I would certainly have advised him to stop. God knows what these unscrupulous, so-called herbalists add to their medicines they peddle to desperate people. I became suspicious at the amount of hair Smyth was losing, but it was too late then."

Jason's hand tensed around the bottle.

"It wouldn't have helped the poor fellow much if he had stopped. I ordered an autopsy on Mr. Smyth. He had a cancerous tumor of the stomach and only a few months to live."

"Thank you." Jason drew in a breath to ease his tight chest. "I'll take the bottle with me and pay this herbalist a visit."

"You won't stop these people, though. Once they've found a way to fleece the public they don't let up."

"Unless they're placed behind bars," Jason said bitterly as rage rampaged through him.

"Quite so, but there's no law to enforce it, sadly. One day perhaps."

Jason pocketed the bottle and walked home. Should the poisoning prove to be deliberate, it would have to be handed over to Bow Street for evidence. Tonight, he had other fish to fry in a certain gambling establishment. And he would go armed.

Entering the house, he was informed that Charlie was escorting Miss Groton and her aunt to a concert while Lizzie was dining with the baron. Events were moving forward without him. He buried a sense of disquiet and ran upstairs to change.

Some hours later, Jason walked into the inner sanctum

of the gaming hell in a narrow lane in St. James's. Men and a scattering of women, some ladies and some not, clustered around the tables where the dice game hazard, backgammon, and card games were in play. Two crystal chandeliers cast their heated light over the heads of the gamblers. The windowless rooms were designed to fleece the "pigeons" — those who lost fortunes in the smoky, stale atmosphere, disorientated, and cut off from the outside world. A roar went up as a young lord staggered away, declaring he would shoot himself, after losing his estate in a game of *vingt-et-un*.

It took Jason little time to locate Fred Pomfret, roaming the tables, a cheroot in his hand. Charlie had described the big, hefty man perfectly, his mean face, broken nose, and mane of red hair. He saw Jason and ambled over to him, no doubt judging him to be a plump pigeon and keen to relieve him of his blunt.

"I should like a word with you, Pomfret, somewhere quiet."

Pomfret's eyes narrowed. "I don't believe we've met, Mr....?"

"Peyton." Jason handed him his card.

Pomfret nodded. "Our best French champagne is on offer to those who fought for England, Captain. Require a stake? We can do that too."

"Just lead the way to your office, Pomfret."

With a cautious frown, Pomfret turned and led Jason to a small room. When Pomfret jerked his thumb at the cashier, the man rose and left.

"Now, Captain. What can I do for you?" he asked, adopting a conciliatory tone. "Some young relative of yours got himself into trouble? We aren't nursemaids 'ere."

Jason pulled his coat back to reveal the pistol tucked into his waistband. "The matter concerns a Miss Groton."

Pomfret's frowning gaze roamed from the gun to Jason's face. "We don't allow firearms in 'ere. What about 'er?"

"I am here to collect her father's IOUs."

"You intend to pay his debt?"

"No, I do not. Miss Groton has no way of paying her father's gambling debts, as you well know, and nor *should* she," he said with quiet menace, tamping down the desire to take his fists to the man. "What I will promise is not to make you significantly more nervous."

Pomfret rose on his toes. "I am not afraid of you, milord. I 'ave many good friends in this business."

"Including your partner in this club, Lord Saville?"

Pomfret scowled. "'im too."

"But I happen to know, Pomfret, that you are new to London. Finding your feet as it were. And Lord Saville, who is a member of my club, wishes to keep a low profile regarding his connection to this gambling hell. If your name, linked to his, ends up in the newspapers, that will upset him, and you'll be out on your backside if you're lucky, or dead in some alley if you're not. Surely even Miss Groton isn't worth that. Pretty as she is."

A tick formed in Pomfret's jaw as silence fell.

"Come, Pomfret. Mr. Groton could not owe you much.

He was not a rich man. And it appears you have done well tonight." Jason held out his hand, aware that the prize was not money but Miss Groton. "The vowels if you will."

Pomfret swiveled and went to open a cupboard. Withdrawing a box, he rifled through it and returned with the signed IOUs. "Take 'em. You peers think you can rule it over everyone."

"You work for a peer, Pomfret," Jason reminded him, relieving him of the scraps of paper. "If any more of these turn up, I won't be so polite next time. And I, too, have some very good friends."

~~~

Helen discovered the French lady's maid, Eloise, in her mother's boudoir, attending to one of her mother's hats. With brisk neat stitches, she attached a satin rose to a silk bonnet.

At the mention of Bart, Eloise bowed her head over her work with a deep sigh. "*Je suis vraiment désolée.*"

"Can you remember anything unusual Bart might have said before he became ill?" Helen asked.

Her black eyes grew wide. "*Oui.* Bart believed that something 'e knew would improve 'is situation."

"What was that?"

"I do not know. But he was insistent. After I teased him, he said when he became rich he would ask me to marry him." She shrugged her narrow shoulders. "I can get my way with most things, Lady Helen." She smoothed her mobcap in the mirror. "But he would not tell me this."

Frustrated, Helen left the room. It would be difficult to believe anything Eloise said. It wasn't that she told lies, but she was given to dramatics.

Downstairs in the servants' quarters, Jeremy had just returned from running a message. Helen drew him aside. "Did Bart say or do anything that surprised you in the weeks before he died?"

The tall footman flushed and shuffled his feet. "No, Lady Helen."

"You won't be in any trouble, Jeremy. But I need to know."

He scratched his head. "Just that he asked me to watch out for him while he went into the library. The family was out. I knew it was wrong, Lady Helen, but he was insistent."

"When was this?"

"A few weeks ago, now."

"What was he looking for?"

"Refused to say. Said it was better if I didn't know."

"Did he remove anything from the library?"

"I didn't see it if he did, but when he put his hand on my shoulder to thank me, he was shaking like one of Cook's jellies. Went straight up to his room. Said he had a letter to write."

"Think carefully, Jeremy. Is there anything else you can tell me?"

"Bart asked me to deliver the letter for him, as it was my afternoon off."

"Where did you take it?"

Jeremy's gaze darted away from hers. "Whitehall, Lady Helen. Fair put the wind up me, it did."

"It's good that you told me. But you have no reason to worry. That will be all, thank you, Jeremy."

After the footman hurried away to return to his duties, Helen, worried about the reason Bart felt it necessary to write to the government, made her way to the kitchen. But it made Peyton's explanation more believable. Surprised at the extent of her relief, she entered the kitchen. The kitchen maids bobbed a welcome, but as she was often here discussing recipes with Cook, they continued with their work. Jinx, the young kitchen boy, greeted her, pausing from his task of peeling potatoes at the big scrubbed wooden table. As Cook was in the larder taking an inventory, Helen slipped into a chair.

"Are you fully recovered, Jinx?"

His narrow face was still pale beneath his freckles. "Yes, thank you, Lady Helen."

"Do you remember anything you and Bart might have shared? A drink or a sweetmeat, some food, which could have made you sick?"

"No, we just ate the meals Cook prepared for us as we always do."

"No one else felt ill?"

"They didn't say so, Lady Helen."

"And there was nothing you and Bart shared? Think, Jinx."

"Only a spoonful of Bart's tonic, if that is what you mean. He said it would cure my cold. Tasted something awful and I spat most of it out."

Her heart thudding, Helen rose from the table. "Please ask Mrs. Chance to advise me if you feel ill again."

Deep in thought, she returned to the upper floor. The information she'd gained posed more questions than answers. Why would anyone want to poison Bart? Perhaps he had known he was in danger when he'd written to the government requesting his captain's help. In what capacity did Lord Peyton work for the government? Could he be a spy? She drew in a breath at the fluttery feeling in her belly. How little they knew about him.

In the unoccupied library, she hurried over to her father's desk. His secretary had a small office at the rear of the house but spent most of his days here in her father's absence. Her father preferred to work in the library. He liked to roam about studying his antiquities. Helped a man to think, he said.

She searched the desk, but it proved a waste of time. So many papers and portfolios, some written in foreign languages, and she had no idea what she was looking for, except those two words, which were unlikely to leap out at her.

She turned as the door opened. "May I assist you, Lady Helen?" Mr. Thorburn blinked behind his glasses. He reminded her of a friendly animal in a storybook she read to Alexander. With a smile, he crossed to where she stood behind the desk.

Thorburn had been her father's faithful and discreet

secretary for several years. Helen thought to ask him if he knew anything about *electric fish*. But remembering Peyton's advice to be discreet, she turned back to the desk. "Just a new pen, thank you, Mr. Thorburn." She picked one up and, smiling, left the room.

Out in the corridor, she paused to consider what she'd learned. It seemed unlikely that the tonic had been accidentally poisoned unless a mistake had been made by the herbalist. Why would anyone deliberately tamper with it with the intention of harming Bart? But there was that letter to the government he'd written, she reminded herself, which pointed to something more sinister. She was eager to pass on to Lord Peyton what she'd learned. But thinking of his perceptive green eyes, she expected he already knew it.

CHAPTER EIGHT

"I can't believe you got hold of these so easily, Jas."
Charlie thumbed through the pile of IOUs during breakfast.
"Amelia will be most grateful." He grinned. "I wish I'd been
there to see it. How did you do it, Jas?"

Jason shrugged. "Just a little reverse blackmail. What
will Miss Groton decide to do? Return to Oxford?"

Charlie stabbed a kidney on his plate with his fork,
releasing a tasty aroma. "Good heavens, no. She loves
London. I've promised to take her driving in Hyde Park
today. I thought the high perch phaeton with the grays. It's
an opportunity to show her how skilled I am with the reins."

Jason was aware of Charlie's desire to become known as
a notable whip. But he had yet to learn discernment. "Take
the curricle, Charlie." He was unsure his nerves could
withstand Charlie demonstrating his skills in the phaeton,
an unstable carriage at best, and tempted to spring the
horses while driving around the park.

Charlie looked crestfallen. "Rather a tame vehicle, Jas."

"Is it? I believe all the young bucks prefer it because it's light and fast."

"Fast, eh? Right you are then."

Charlie finished his breakfast at great speed. "I'm off to the stables and can hardly wait to tell Miss Groton the good news."

Jason eyed his brother's broad back as he hurried from the room. He was a good-looking young man. Would Miss Groton resist the attraction? It would be a test of her character should she be swayed by a prospective beau who was plumper in the pocket. Jason sighed. Life was filled with disappointments, but even so, he would hate to see Charlie hurt.

He took up the broadsheet but mused over what he'd learned about Bart's death. He'd sent a note to Bow Street and expected a runner to be assigned to the case. He hoped it would be one of their best men. Bow Street didn't always work well with the government.

A sensitive handling of this was required, for it appeared that the answer lay within the walls of Kinsey House. Despite his warning, might Lady Helen take it upon herself to discover what had happened to Bart? Such a possibility was unnerving and made him put aside the newspaper. He would be relieved when her father returned home. Until then the family was vulnerable. Lady Kinsey was smart, but a woman's power was limited, and Toby, as the only male member in residence, was just fifteen.

He'd have a word with the watchman and urge him to keep a sharp eye out when he called on Lady Kinsey tomorrow. Today, he planned to seek out the herbalist named on the bottle.

As he drank a final cup of strong coffee, bitter the way he liked it, Lizzie entered in a lavender and cream striped walking gown. "That color becomes you, Lizzie," he observed. "You're up early this morning."

"I am to assist the baron with the placement of several paintings that have just arrived in London." She poured a cup of tea from the fresh pot brought by the footman.

Jason knew it would be a waste of time advising her to take her maid. "I gather the exhibition goes well thus far?"

Her eyes brightened. "Jas, I can't wait for you to see the fine art the baron has brought to England." She shrugged. "Although I suspect I am not a great deal of help to him. He insists that I am. While we consider the best arrangement for the paintings, he talks always of his home in Florence. Statues amongst the aged cypress trees, groves of olives, and grape-laden arbors. And the sunshine. So very different to England. It does sound appealing."

"You have been seen alone with him now on several occasions. Has he made his intentions clear?"

A small frown creased her forehead. "Not precisely."

"Take care, Lizzie."

"Widows don't come under as much scrutiny as unmarried girls. And what the gossips might think doesn't concern me. He may not want to marry me. After all, there's no guarantee I'll give him an heir."

"Isn't that so for every woman? Who's to say the problem didn't lie with Greywood."

She flushed and shook her head, unwilling to find any fault with her dead husband. "But the fact remains that Greywood and I were childless after five years of marriage. It may sway Bianchi's decision." Her eyes darkened. "I enjoy being with him, Jas. I feel happier than I have for ages. Is that so very bad?"

He reached across and patted her hand where it moved restlessly on the table. "I understand your need to find love again."

"Do you?" Lizzie proceeded to butter her toast. She eyed him thoughtfully. "Why don't you believe in marriage?"

"I haven't seen many good marriages to persuade me."

"You are thinking of our parents."

"That is one example, certainly. It seemed to me that Father was more content after Mother was gone."

Lizzie paused, her spoon hovering over the pot of marmalade. "That's not true! He was miserable! You didn't see it. You weren't there very much."

"I was there in the early days, Lizzie. You were a baby. You didn't witness the rows, the threats, the smashing of ornaments. Father riding off for hours alone." Recalling it saddened him. "But toward the end, he seemed peaceful."

She spread jam over the toast. "Theirs was a fiery, passionate relationship."

"Well, I would never want that."

"You did want to marry, once." She took a bite and chewed pensively. "Does your reluctance have anything to do with Phoebe?"

Phoebe. They had both been so young and thought they

had the whole of their lives ahead of them. He drew in a deep breath. "That was a long time ago."

Lizzie gave him a careful glance. "It was such a tragedy when she was thrown from her horse."

"She was always a neck-or-nothing rider. Shouldn't have been riding Juno, her father's stallion, let alone jumping him over that brick wall." The memory still had the power to tighten his throat, although it had lessened over the years, leaving him with profound regret. After Phoebe had ignored his appeal, he should have pulled her off that skittish horse. He'd gone after her, but too late.

"You joined the army almost immediately after her death," she said. "Father was furious."

"He was at the time." Father had said he'd never forgive him. He'd accused Jason of letting the family down. Father had Charlie, Jason had argued, but it fell on deaf ears. In the following years, when he'd returned from the army intact, physically, at least, they'd made peace with one another, and their relationship had been a cordial one when his father died.

"You and Phoebe practically grew up together, on neighboring estates. I can well understand if her death has left a hole in your heart. But that doesn't mean you should go through life alone."

Lizzie made him uncomfortable, forcing him to take a close look at himself. She was one of a few who could. He fought to distract her, raising an eyebrow. "I'm not a monk."

"Bah! What of mistresses, they care little for their

patrons, beyond what they can get from them."

"They have to make their way in this hazardous world too. But I refuse to discuss the merits or otherwise of mistresses. I believe I know what is best for me." He pushed away his plate. "Think very carefully about what you want for yourself. A man such as Bianchi may be personable, more demonstrative than an English woman is used to, perhaps. But finding yourself alone in Florence may not be so charming if the baron isn't quite what he appears."

With a scowl, she leaned back in her chair. "I believe we've had this conversation. Are you making inquiries about him, Jas?"

"It's my responsibility as head of the family." He wanted to say more, that he acted out of love and concern for her, but before he could explain, she'd thrown back her chair and left the room.

Sighing, he slowly followed in her wake. He had expected it to come to this.

~~~

The ball gowns had been delivered. Diana insisted Helen come to their bedchamber to try them on.

"Oh, they're exquisite!" Helen gasped with pleasure as Mary assisted her into her gown. While Mary tugged at the hooks, Helen studied herself in the cheval mirror. It was quite the prettiest gown she'd ever worn. Of white lace over a lilac satin slip, the tight-fitting bodice featured a deep square neckline decorated with a narrow rouleau, the skirt embroidered with a broad pattern of flowers and leaves and a matching rouleau puffed and corded around the hem.

Mary turned her attentions to Diana. The simple but artfully designed white muslin was perfect. Flowers embroidered in silk thread decorated the deep, square neckline, stiffened hem, and puff sleeves.

"We each have a beaded reticule to complement our gowns." Diana's eyes sparkled. "And satin shoes. Mine are white, and yours are lilac." She removed everything from the boxes, silver paper strewn around.

Helen was caught by her reflection. She frowned and placed a hand on her chest. "Perhaps this needs more lace."

Diana stood beside her. "Goose. It is perfectly presentable, or Mama would have told Madame Fabre to alter it."

"I suppose so," Helen said. "I must remember not to take a deep breath."

Diana giggled. "You do look quite lovely; the color makes your skin glow."

"I never liked myself in white."

"White doesn't suit everyone," Diana said, turning to view the back of her gown in the mirror. "I think it's unkind to insist girls wear white when they wish to make a good first impression. I shall wear pastels after the ball, but I look my best in a more dramatic color, such as bright yellow or crimson."

Helen grinned. "Oh, no, not crimson! Not until you're an old married lady."

Mama opened the door. "You look beautiful, both of

you, but take them off, please, and allow Mary to put the gowns away. It wouldn't do to have them look shabby before you even have a chance to wear them."

Shame-faced, Diana hurried over to Mary. "Yes, Mama."

Mama perched on the bed, her eyes on Helen. "We are expecting a visitor tomorrow. Lord Peyton is to call."

"Oh, good," Diana said in a muffled voice as the maid carefully pulled the gown over her head. "I hoped to see him again."

"But not tomorrow, Diana. This is not a social call," Mama said. "I would like you to attend, Helen. He may have questions only you can answer."

Diana emerged from the gown with a grimace and stood in her chemise, corset, and drawers. "What more can be said about poor Bart now he is in his grave?"

"We shall see. Shall I ask your father to invite Peyton to the ball?" Mama's eyes twinkled. "I consider him more than capable of wrestling the other gentlemen away for a dance with you."

Apparently mollified, Diana kissed their mother's cheek.

Helen turned her back for Mary to undo her gown, trying to ignore the little skip in the region of her heart. Should Peyton come to the ball, would he ask her to dance? It surprised her how much she wanted him to. After all, one dance could hardly matter to anyone but her. Or would she be relegated to the corner where the wallflowers gathered, some of who had become friends over the years? She no longer feared such a thing. It had become a refuge of sorts. After the gossip of her first Season had died down, and she'd rejected two suitors who made it plain they were taking her on sufferance, there were only the fortune hunters or widowed gentlemen in need of a governess for their children who exhibited any interested in her, and they were given short shrift by her father.

CHAPTER NINE

Jason increased his pace as dark clouds clustered
overhead and the early torrential rain threatened to return.
Water dripped down the brick walls and formed pools in the
narrow lanes of Whitechapel. The dank smell of mold,
blended with the stink of cats and human detritus,
intensified, strong enough to make his eyes sting.

A bell tinkled as Jason pushed open the door of Mr.
Frank's establishment. Hardly a flourishing business, paint
peeled from the woodwork, the interior grim and badly lit,
the shelves on the walls poorly stocked. A curtain was
dragged aside, and a man stepped into the room. Not very
old, Jason guessed, but he didn't appear robust, his grayish
skin tones not a good advertisement for his tonic. He
nodded to Jason and rested his hands on the counter. "May I
help you, sir?"

Jason handed him his card then pulled the empty bottle
from his coat pocket. "I believe that a Mr. Bartholomew
Smyth purchased this from you."

"I wouldn't remember the gentleman. I sell so many of
them." He reached out and took the bottle. "That's one of

ours. A popular item."

"What is in it?"

He pushed out his chest. "That's a secret, milord. I'm not about to have it duplicated by others."

"I shouldn't think you would, seeing as it killed Mr. Smyth."

His pale eyes widened with alarm. "Killed him? No, indeed. That's not possible. There's nothing in my elixir to harm anyone."

"There's arsenic in it," Jason said. "Enough to slowly kill Mr. Smyth within a matter of weeks."

Frank shook his head violently. "Not in my nerve tonic, sir!" He reached behind him and removed an identical bottle from the shelf. After removing the lid, he put the bottle to his lips and drank. He slammed the bottle down and beat his chest. "As you see I am still hale and hearty. Would I take such a risk if I believed it to contain arsenic?"

"May I examine its contents?"

"You may do what you wish with it. Take it away and test it. You won't find arsenic in it. You must look elsewhere for the explanation of Mr. Smyth's death, God rest his soul. Did he suffer any hair loss?"

"I believe so."

Frank nodded. "If arsenic was in it, I did not put it there. I'm not in the business of killing my customers. I use beef blood, marrow, and salt, mixed with water and a little alcohol, to strengthen the body and heal the nerves."

"Could it have been in the water?"

"Absolutely not! I use pure rainwater, which I collect

myself. Nor do I add opiates, as they are contrary to my philosophy. If there's arsenic in this, it would smell of bitter almonds." Frank pushed the bottle he'd drunk from across the counter. "No trace of it. Care to try?"

Jason waved it under his nose. It smelled as Mr. Frank had suggested, of salty beef and the faint tang of cheap gin.

"I suggest that arsenic was added to that gentleman's tonic after he bought it. If I may be so bold. I hope this won't get around, milord," Franks added, his hands clenched on the countertop. "It would destroy my business."

"Not unless you are found to have destroyed your customers' health with your tonics, Mr. Frank. If you did, you can expect a visit from the Watch. Good day."

Jason pocketed the bottles, deciding whether to give the new one to the surgeon to test. But he was already convinced that Bart's was not an accidental death.

~~~

When Helen entered the drawing room, she found Lord Peyton in conversation with her mother. He rose to his feet with a smile.

As she greeted him, her heart gave another little skip. It was perplexing that he, of all people, could awaken something in her that had lain dormant for years. Especially, when Diana was determined to ensnare him. But did Peyton intend to marry? She'd never seen him at Almack's, that select establishment nicknamed the marriage mart she'd attended with her family over the years. Or any of the debutante balls she'd suffered through. And she was sure she would remember him, as wallflowers observed far more than those on the dance floor. She sat down beside her mother on the sofa.

Today, Peyton had teamed a gray suit of superfine with a white waistcoat embroidered in silver leaves, his cravat tied in a simple knot. She admired his careless grace as he rested his long fingers on the arms of the chair, crossed his ankles encased in gleaming leather, and smiled at her.

His smile was so warm she couldn't help smiling back.

"So, Lady Helen. Lady Kinsey informs me you have been questioning the staff. Have you anything new to tell me?"

She relayed her scant information. "I realize it's not particularly helpful," she said finally. "Perhaps you have learned something of significance?"

He raised his eyebrows, possibly at her presumption. "As I have told your mother, it appears that the tonic bottle was tampered with after it was purchased."

A chill rushed through her veins. "By someone in this house?"

"That remains a possibility, of course, although there is no conclusive evidence." He uncrossed his ankles and leaned forward. "I understand Lady Diana's ball will keep the family in London. Lady Helen, although I do appreciate your assistance during this investigation, it would be wise for you to leave this matter to Bow Street and to me."

"Yes, Helen. What Lord Peyton is saying, diplomatically, is that it could be dangerous if you were to take it upon yourself to uncover the truth." Mama gasped and put a hand to her breast, as their perilous circumstances suddenly became clear. "It is unthinkable that we might have a murderer in our midst. We might be slain in our beds!"

"Too many unknown factors remain to jump to that conclusion, my lady," Peyton said. "One possible consideration is that the tonic was tampered with somewhere else. Do not be too distressed, I beg of you. I shall be on hand to help. If anything happens to worry you, you need only send word."

When Peyton spoke with cool authority Helen's panic lessened, but her questions remained unanswered. "What about the burned fragment of letter containing those strange words, *electric fish*?"

"I imagine your father is better able to answer that. It may bear no relevance at all to Bart's death."

Fiske entered the room, followed by Jeremy with the tea tray. "Excuse me, my lady, but Mrs. Chance is interviewing the extra staff required for the ball. She apologizes and asks if you may be able to spare a moment."

Her mother stood. "Please excuse me, my lord. Helen will entertain you."

The door closed. Helen, her pulse thudding at finding herself alone with him, seized the teapot and busied herself. "I believe you take milk, my lord?"

"I do, thank you."

Helen placed the cup and saucer patterned with flowers on the table before him. She moved the laden cake stand closer to him. "Would you care for a sandwich, lemon cake…" Her mind became blank when she met his quizzical gaze. "Cook makes very good coconut macaroons." What was it about him that stripped her of her composure with one glance?

"I shall sample everything." A smile tugged at his lips. He placed two tiny ham and cress sandwiches and two macaroons on his plate. As he stirred sugar into his tea, his gaze caught hers again. "Tell me what interests you, Lady Helen."

"My interests, my lord?" Startled, Helen took something from the platter as she attempted an answer, and then she discovered it was the lemon cake, which was not to her taste. She could hardly put it back so left it on her plate. She took a deep breath and regained her wits. "I find the exhibits at the museum quite fascinating. Many of my father's discoveries are there. Reading, too, and long walks when in the country." Picking crabapples for Cook to make preserves while Bertie, their terrier, barked at the finches feeding on the yew berries. Peyton would hardly wish to hear that. "Cherrywood, the family's cozy old house in Kent, is beautiful with the walls and the chimneys covered in great splashes of crimson Virginia creeper."

"I can imagine. Nothing better than the countryside in spring," he agreed.

She supposed he would prefer to ride. On horseback, he must look quite splendid. Helen almost sighed aloud. "I do look forward to returning there with the family, playing charades or whist after dinner." It would not be that way for very long. Diana would marry, Toby would go off to university, and Harry would take digs in Town...

She glanced up at Peyton from under her lashes as he ate a macaroon. He would not want to hear how she baked cakes in the big country kitchen stove, testing recipes Cook gave her. He would consider her prosaic, which she undoubtedly was. But what else could she say? That she was a keen skater when the pond froze over and played the piano and sang for musical evenings? These activities were unlikely to impress him. A man such as he, who had lived a full life and worked in some secret capacity for the government, perhaps as a spy, would want an exciting woman. That was the way of the world.

"I spend as much time as I can at my country seat, Peyton Grove, in Surrey," he said.

"You have family there?"

"Not now."

Wasn't he lonely? She was curious but could hardly ask him. And she supposed he couldn't be, or he would marry.

"You don't speak of London," he said, disconcerting her. "Do you not enjoy the Season?"

She should have expected the question. Her shortcomings were unfortunately too obvious. But she refused to embellish and pretend to be what she was not. "The theater and the opera and walking in Hyde Park."

Helen bit her lip and prodded the offending cake with a fork, spreading its contents over her plate. She longed to come up with something thrilling, to see interest spark in his eyes. But had no expectation of it. "I beat my brother, Harry, at chess, and he says he was considered quite accomplished at university." She smiled, remembering how Harry always blustered. "Toby says Harry swells up like a bullfrog. It does make him rather cross."

He laughed. "Then I am in sympathy with him. My sister, Lizzie, is a whiz at faro. I would rather you didn't put that about, though. It might ruin my reputation at White's."

The mellow timber of his chuckle sent tingles down her spine. "I've met your sister, Elizabeth," she said, forking up a piece of cake and taking a hurried sip of tea. Cook always made it too sweet.

Peyton finished his second coconut macaroon. "You don't enjoy dancing?"

"Oh, yes. I do. I love to dance." She assumed he was trying to understand her. Most likely was perplexed by her. She was glad to offer something that might make her seem more like all the young women he would have met. But dances meant balls, which she hated. She sighed. "I'm afraid you must find me exceedingly dull, my lord."

"*Au contraire*, Lady Helen."

She risked a look in his eyes and was startled to find a gleam in them. Did he find her amusing?

Her mother's return saved her from dwelling on the question.

"Do forgive me, the amount of organization that goes into holding a ball is astonishing! Now, where were we?" She took the cup of tea Helen had poured for her. "Please use the library for your interviews, Lord Peyton. Fiske shall send Jeremy and my maid, Eloise, to you after your tea. I'm afraid Mrs. Chance is about to leave. You might speak to her tomorrow. Helen, you must assist his lordship with anything he requires."

The conversation turned to more mundane matters until the tea tray was removed and Fiske escorted Peyton to the library.

Mama gazed at her. "What did you and his lordship speak of in my absence?"

"He inquired about my interests. I expect I bored him."

"I very much doubt it."

Helen wanted to ask what her mother meant, but Fiske interrupted them. "A letter has come, my lady. I thought it best to bring it to you immediately."

"Thank you, Fiske." Mama opened and studied it. "It's from your father. It appears his boat has docked safely in Liverpool. His departure will be delayed while he attends to business. He must arrange a consignment to be shipped to London." She put the letter down in her lap with a relieved sigh. "It's to be hoped he'll soon be home. How good it will be to see him."

"Yes, Mama." Helen wondered how her mother bore her father's long absences. Mama had once traveled with Papa to Constantinople but became quite ill in the heat. After that, she seemed content to remain at home and continue with her charities.

Helen yearned to visit exotic climes. She hoped that after a few years had passed, and her mother became resigned to her not marrying, they might allow her to accompany her father and assist him in his work. She did not express her wish now, however, because they would never believe her, and she knew it would cause a ruckus. Patience was required for timing was everything.

Her mother tucked the letter in her pocket. "Please go and see if his lordship requires anything, Helen."

Was Mama pushing her in Peyton's direction? She wanted to question her, but there was little point, for if she was, Helen knew the reason. Mama considered Helen spending time with a personable man to be a curative If only it was that simple.

CHAPTER TEN

Jason was glad to find Kinsey's secretary, Thorburn, absent from the library. He had no intention of including Thorburn in this investigation, as he remained high on the list of suspects.

He had learned nothing from the male members of the staff. The nervous footman, Jeremy, had been remarkably unobservant, considering his bedroom was next door to Bart's.

"Only the muffled voice of Mrs. Chance, who tended to him. Very efficiently too," Jeremy had said. "Kept him as clean and comfortable as was possible. And quite firm with the staff. Wouldn't allow us to stay long unless we upset him, but poor Bart was too ill to notice that we were there."

Disheartened, Jason had hoped for more. The maids' chambers were segregated from the men's, situated in a different wing. Fiske also had rooms at the opposite end of the corridor to Bart's and was no help at all, apart from expressing sorrow that he'd chastised Bart for his negligent appearance.

"I heard Bart arguing with Mrs. Chance," one of the upstairs maids, Alice, her eyes like saucers, whispered in a conspiratorial manner when he questioned her. "It shocked me to hear him speak like that, so I stopped and listened."

"When was this?"

"A week or so before he took to his bed, milord."

"What was the argument about?"

"Mrs. Chance wanted him to run an errand, and he refused. Bart said something I didn't understand."

"And what was that, Alice?"

"Bart said, 'You must think me a fool.'"

"That was all?"

Alice chewed her bottom lip. "Yes, milord. Mrs. Chance told him to be careful. He might find himself out on the street without a character."

"What do you think Bart meant by that?"

"When Mrs. Chance had gone away, I asked him. He just said he didn't like to go on personal errands for her."

"But footmen are required to run messages for the house, are they not?"

"Yes, milord. And when I reminded him of it, he just shrugged."

The French lady's maid was of no help at all. After reminiscing about how she and Bart conversed in French, she fell upon Jason's chest in tears.

After calming Eloise, he sent her down to the kitchen for a cup of tea.

When Lady Helen entered the room, he was studying artifacts in a glass-fronted cabinet. Jason turned to her.

"Your father has an excellent collection." He watched her cross the room, coolly composed. He'd begun to suspect she donned her unruffled demeanor like steel-plated armor, and he wondered why. It could not always have been so, for he caught glimpses beneath the façade. He had no business wondering, of course, and wished he could stop. But each time he saw her, he came away wanting to know more.

"Yes. Although Papa donates most of his discoveries to the museum."

He paused before a decorative detail depicting two donkeys bearing loads. "Didn't the Ancient Egyptians have camels? They are known to be the ships of the desert, are they not?"

"Not then, no, they preferred donkeys. And wooden barges on the Nile to move grain and stone blocks. They used the Nile like we do our roads, sailing in papyrus boats." She smiled at him, and for once, he could see her relax into herself. When she glanced up toward the blue-painted ceiling above them, he caught a glimpse of the dewy magnolia skin of her throat, which looked petal soft. "And every day, high above the river, the sun god Ra was believed to sail across the sky in his solar boat."

"I don't blame them for forgoing camels. They look like fractious beasts, and very uncomfortable."

She laughed, making him grin at how infectious it was. "I hope to ride one."

"You do?" He wondered at that and tried to imagine it but failed. This starchy young lady on a camel? "I can't quite see it," he said, his lips twitching.

She shrugged, looking annoyed. "I don't see why. Is it because I'm a woman?"

"I can assure you it isn't," he hastened to say, enjoying the fire in her eyes. "I believe camels would be deliberately bad-mannered with both sexes."

Her eyes danced. "Women do travel to exotic climes. Do you know that Egyptian women had equal rights with men?"

"They did?" He wanted to prolong the discussion, enjoying her animation. This conversation brought Lady Helen out of where she'd been hiding. And for that, he was both intrigued and grateful.

"Yes. Men and women were treated as equals in the eyes of the law. Unlike today," she said with an exasperated shrug, "women could own, earn, buy, sell, and inherit property. They could live unprotected by male guardians and, if widowed or divorced, could raise their own children. They could bring cases before, and be punished by, the law courts."

"Were they not expected to marry?"

"Yes, and the wife was the mistress of the house, responsible for domestic matters. She raised the children while their husband provided for them."

"Not so different to today, then," he said, teasing her.

"Marriage today is very different, Lord Peyton," she said crisply. "A wife has no rights and loses any claim to property."

"Not all men are tyrants, Lady Helen. Some allow their wives a good deal of freedom. You surely must agree."

"My father certainly, who is a cut above most men. But while these laws remain, women will never be free."

"Only your father, Lady Helen? Surely, you have met decent men since you entered society?"

"I don't believe we were discussing my circumstances." Her lashes hid her expression, and the Helen who spoke to him as a confident equal and challenged him was gone.

He wanted to better understand her but had been too forthright. He moved on to view a Greek vase then discovered naked men cavorting in imaginative ways around its circumference. Lady Helen flicked a disinterested glance at the detailed, suggestive poses and stepped away. He almost smiled, suspecting she'd examined it quite closely when it first arrived. But fearing he might offend her, he turned his attention to a base-relief of Egyptian hieroglyphs. "I viewed the Rosetta Stone in the British Museum. The English army recovered it from the French during the Egyptian campaign in 1801."

"A very important find," she said at his elbow, "as it's hoped to hold the key to deciphering hieroglyphic language."

"Indeed." He turned to observe her bright, intelligent eyes and wished he didn't have to return to the matter at hand. "I have yet to speak with your housekeeper. Is Mrs. Chance away for the afternoon?"

"Yes, she is visiting her brother."

"He lives in London?"

"He travels a good deal for his work. She always has the afternoon off when he's in the city."

"What can you tell me about Mr. Thorburn?"

"My father likes him. He has worked as Papa's secretary for a few years."

"I need to see him. He doesn't have quarters in the

house?"

"No. Neither does he work on Mondays."

Jason had avoided approaching Kinsey's desk and rifling through his papers, but he spied the earl's handsome magnifying glass perched on a brass and polished wooden stand. He reached into his pocket. "Shall we examine the letter fragment?"

She drew in a breath. "Oh yes, let's."

Removing the scrap from his wallet he placed the fragile paper carefully onto the polished surface of the desk and bent to examine it through the magnifying glass. A few of the letters leaped out at him. "Interesting."

"What is? Let me see." She moved closer, her delicate perfume reminding him of early spring. Her hair brushed his wrist as she lowered her head to peer through the glass at the smudged words. Distracted, he breathed her in. *She must wash her hair with lavender soap.* She raised her head, her gray eyes questioning. "I believe I can make out more of the first line."

"Tell me what you see," he said, held captive by her sudden arresting smile.

"I think this is, 'Abused Lord…and this 'Kin,' but the rest is blurred. Surely this must refer to my father. It wasn't 'truth' as we'd previously thought. It's 'trust.' My father's trust has been abused?"

"I thought the same. It doesn't tell us much, except that the letter concerns your father. It appears we must be patient until we can consult him."

A book titled *Description De l'Égypte* perched on the

desk. Opening it, he found it to be a catalog of interesting notes, engravings, and drawings from over a hundred scholars and scientists.

"It was collated at Napoleon's decree and covers all aspects of ancient and modern Egypt and its natural history," she said, leaning back against the desk to watch him.

He turned the page. "Fascinating."

"I find it so."

"You've read this?"

A flash of humor crossed her face. "I am working my way through it."

He glanced at her in admiration. Lady Helen was proving fascinating herself.

Beside the book were notes written in Arabic. Although he could read Latin and Greek, his grasp of Arabian script was limited. But one name stood out because it was written in English. "Has your father ever mentioned a Mr. Alexandro Volta?"

She searched his eyes, hers turning a brilliant gray-blue, like crushed violets. "No, why?"

Startled by the change in her, those remarkable eyes, and that delicately flushed skin, Jason fought to order his thoughts. "I remember reading something about Volta. Now, what was it? Ah yes. He was awarded the Copley by the Royal Society of London for his scientific research. Invented a glowing wire, I believe. One of the many experiments concerning magnetic and electrical power."

She gasped, her eyes alight, seemingly unaware that her hand clutched his sleeve. "It could have some connection to electric fish!"

His gaze dropped to her luscious lips. "I believe you're right!" Without thought, he leaned forward and pressed a brief kiss on her mouth.

Somehow, the kiss lengthened. Her mouth softened under his, and she made a small appreciative noise as his arm swept around her waist to pull her closer. He became aware of the soft compliant body within his arm, and the luscious taste of her lips, and his blood rampaged through his veins.

She stiffened, and he pulled away, dropping his hands.

"My lord!" She gave a shaky laugh, her hand to her mouth, and stepped back.

"Forgive me," he said with a shameless grin, his blood still pounding. "This is not something I normally do, kissing ladies on brief acquaintance. An impulse. I blame the excitement of the moment."

What a disgraceful fellow he was. Not only had he broken every rule of etiquette, he'd lied. He didn't regret kissing her one bit. She'd looked so vividly alive and quite beautiful, and he couldn't resist. But she'd be well within her rights to slap him.

She did not. Her cheeks flamed, and her tongue traced her lips. What he hadn't expected was his own reaction to the touch and taste of her, and the heat that streaked through him, making him want to draw her close again and kiss her senseless. He cleared his throat.

"I should go. I'm confident Lord Kinsey will enlighten us."

"Yes...yes. I believe he will." Doubt clouded her eyes

like a summer storm.

"I'll interview your housekeeper tomorrow. You expect your father home on time?"

"He has been delayed for a few days," she said over her shoulder and hurried to the door as if he was about to pounce on her.

Jason watched her uneasily. He had not experienced that reaction from a lady before. He cursed himself for his rash behavior, although he still could not regret the kiss.

Walking home, despite the interesting connection to Volta, Jason could think of nothing but Lady Helen. How her feisty, confident manner, so very different to her careful demeanor, had aroused something in him he didn't quite understand. He'd wanted to draw closer, which surprised him as much as her. She returned his kiss in a very un-spinster-like manner, her hands resting on his shoulders before she pushed him away. But still, it was clear she did not welcome his attentions. Irritated by a rash action that seemed most unlike him, he hoped there would be no awkwardness between them when they met again. He did not normally act impulsively, and certainly not with a lady he respected.

A letter from his university friend, Robert Vale, who was in Italy, awaited him. Jason went to the library to read it. Vale was now studying art in Florence under one of the masters. He had exhibited considerable artistic talent at university, but his passion had distracted him from his studies, and he'd failed his exams.

They'd spent Robert's last evening drinking ale in an Oxford tavern while he explained why he wasn't in the least sorry to be leaving university and how a man's expectations of where he stood in the world were often blinkered. Jason still remembered his words, "Sometimes, the beliefs you carry throughout life are simply wrong, dear fellow."

As they grew more foxed by the hour, Jason had sought to argue, sad to see his friend leave England. Their top-heavy drinking session had occurred only a month after Phoebe died, and Jason had espoused his strongly held opinion that a man who allowed himself to love a woman too deeply was vulnerable to great loss. He now regretted having bored his friend, but he had not changed his mind. Better to move lightly through life and resist temptations like Lady Helen.

It was good that Robert still appeared contented with his life. Jason had had the opportunity to visit him when in Italy. He'd found his artistic friend, who came from a titled and wealthy English family, living in a small house with the voluptuous and excitable mother of their four bambinos.

Jason admitted that, at the time, he'd considered Vale to be hiding from life and avoiding his responsibilities. But reading his letter, he saw he'd been wrong.

Francesca and the children are in good health, and we are soon to welcome another bambino, Vale wrote. *We must now move to a bigger house. A nuisance when we are so comfortable here. Fortunately, I have received a good commission for a portrait, so money is not as tight as it is sometimes. Life is good, my friend. The food is abundant, the sun still shines, and the vino is excellent. You should come to visit and wet the baby's head. As to your Baron Bianchi, I have met him briefly and been privileged to visit his wonderful villa to view his marvelous collection of sculpture and paintings. While I cannot claim to know him intimately, he is well thought of here.*

Putting down the letter, Jason studied the Claude Lorraine landscape of a fictional Italy on the wall opposite. Was Lizzie about to disappear from his life? They'd always been close confidantes who supported each other through the darkest times. Only she understood how his past had affected him. He'd enjoyed her company after Greywood charged him with the task of caring for her. Was that about to change? One could never be sure of what lay in the future. Surely, this reinforced his view of the vagaries of life and how advisable it was to move through it unencumbered.

The door opened, and his brother strode in.

"I missed you last evening, Charlie. How was the theater?"

Charlie flung himself down on the leather sofa. "Mrs. Groton and Amelia found it entertaining, but if you've seen one, you've seen them all." He shrugged. "Tumblers or a juggler's feats are really only astonishing the first time you view them."

Detecting the sour note in Charlie's voice, Jason sat back and viewed him. "What has occurred?"

"Eh? Nothing. Not really." He huffed out a breath. "It's just that when driving Amelia in the park, the dandies and fops clustered around the curricle, demanding to know who she was. And then at the theater, it was even worse."

"Miss Groton is very pretty. You must expect it, Charlie."

"But Amelia encourages them. She's a shocking flirt. Her aunt does nothing to stop her."

"All this is new to her. And very exciting, I imagine."

"I suppose so," Charlie said in a sulky voice. "But she

refused my invitation to go to the opera this evening. Said she had a sore throat and was tired."

"Well, perhaps she is."

He scowled. "I'd be prepared to place a bet in White's betting book that she has another engagement. There was one persistent fellow hanging around her like a bee around the lavender. Didn't like the cut of his jib. Whispered something in her ear I didn't hear."

"Care to go out with me tonight, then?" Jason asked, wishing to distract himself from a vision of Lady Helen in his arms. "I'm happy for you to choose the venue, except for cockfights."

Charlie grinned. "Really? That would be grand, Jas. Tonight there's a chance for a fellow to spar with Gentleman John Jackson at his boxing club."

"Excellent. Afterward, we could indulge in a spot of fencing practice at Angelo's Fencing Academy, next door, then end the night with a good lobster dinner at the Royal Saloon in Piccadilly."

"Capital!" Charlie bounded up, Miss Groton apparently forgotten. Jason was pleased with the opportunity to enjoy Charlie's company before he was sent back. He'd been corresponding with an influential friend who had written to the dean on his behalf. Word had come this morning that Charlie was to return to Oxford at the beginning of the next term. But Jason wasn't about to tell him now. No sense in spoiling the evening.

~~~

As she was about to escape into her bedroom, Helen's mother appeared. "Lord Peyton has left, Helen?"

"Yes, Mama." Her pulse was still racing. Peyton had kissed her. She'd been so caught up in the excitement of their possible discovery, had she unwittingly invited his kiss when she placed a hand on his arm? And before she could gain control of herself, she had kissed him back! Did he think her fast? Or was he a rake? She didn't want to believe it of him. Couldn't, not when she could still feel the touch of his lips and his strong manly arms around her and wanted to be alone to relive the moment.

Her mother, who had the instinct of a lioness, grabbed her arm. "Something has occurred?"

Helen dragged in a slow, deep breath. "Yes, we were able to decipher more of the letter. And must now await Papa's return to understand it." She hoped it was enough to put her mother off.

"Come into your room. I want to hear all about it."

Perched on her bed, she tried to present a coherent account of events, except for, of course, the kiss.

"Well, that is interesting," Mama observed. "And best left to Lord Peyton until your father is home." Helen feared a telltale flush was still in evidence, as a worried frown creased her mother's forehead. "I wonder if I should allow you to spend time alone with Peyton. He is an army man after all."

"Oh, Mama! Lord Peyton is a gentleman, worthy of our trust." Helen surprised herself by rushing to his defense, dismayed at the prospect of them no longer working together and losing their new-found intimacy, no matter how utterly disturbing and fruitless it was. However, it wasn't a lie. Peyton was no rake. He'd quickly let her go when she'd come to her senses. She knew only too well what rakehells were capable of. A rake would have laughed at her reaction, kissed her again, and taken other liberties. Peyton was nothing like Albert Lord Lawley, the gentleman, so called, who had ruined her life. She suppressed a shiver. "You cannot always tell a true gentleman by his title."

"Oh, my darling girl." Sitting on Helen's bed, Mama hugged her close. "No, you cannot." Her voice trembled. "I shall never forgive myself for what happened to you that night."

"It was my fault, Mama. I shouldn't have slipped away onto the terrace with Lawley when Lady Fountain distracted you. When he invited me to stroll in the garden, he was so handsome and charming that I trusted him. I was young and foolish, but I'm not anymore. I don't believe I am wrong about Lord Peyton, although it hardly matters." She knew his kiss meant little more than, as he'd explained, a reaction to the excitement of the moment. "He has no interest in marrying me."

"Nevertheless, my dear, I am relieved you can find it in yourself to trust a man again. I see it as a sign that you've recovered and are open to finding a prospective husband this Season."

Helen neither believed the world had changed nor that a rosy future awaited her. But Peyton had found her attractive enough to kiss, which, when she calmed down, made her smile.

Helen left her mother and went downstairs. The shock of that dreadful time had faded with the years. She could face it without flinching and firmly thrust the memories away. Lawley might have forgotten it too, although his anger at what he saw as unfair treatment made it seem unlikely.

She had been bedridden for some weeks following that terrible ball while gossip filled the news sheets and fueled the talk in drawing rooms. Her mother, fearing Helen's spirits had sunk dangerously low, tended her most lovingly. Mama had insisted that Lawley had taken nothing from Helen that mattered, that she was still the same innocent she'd always been. But Helen knew he'd taken far too much that night, every vestige of her confidence, her hopes, and her dreams. His taunting words as he'd ravaged her were etched into her memory, how he'd sneered when she cried and fought him, saying she should welcome his attentions because she wasn't very pretty and said he would have preferred to be with one of the Season's beauties. Struggling with him, she'd hit her head on a stone wall and lost consciousness. She was thankfully unaware of being carried inside by her father to uproar and speculation.

Lawley, a younger son of an impoverished baron, denied everything, saying that the "silly girl" was merely hysterical, but when the *ton* gave him the cut direct, he'd departed for the Continent soon afterward, leaving behind a mountain of debts. As his pockets were to let, it was Mama's opinion that he'd sought to compromise Helen and force the marriage.

Her dreams might still be haunted by his violent act, but she refused to give in to what that man had done to her.

What she might do if she ever came face to face with him again at some society function, she wasn't sure, but fury not distress now drove her. She only hoped she would never find out.

A deep sigh escaped her, and then she straightened her shoulders. She must stop this stupid admiration of Lord Peyton. While he did not fit her notion of a rake, one who seduced innocent young women, he might consider a lady of her age to be eager for a light flirtation. And if that was the case, well, he could think again. Tomorrow, she would treat him as she had learned to treat every gentleman she met in society, with her head held high, as if his kiss was a matter of complete indifference to her..

CHAPTER ELEVEN

At Kinsey House the next day, Fiske's face was even more sober than usual, and a heavy aura of expectation hung in the air. "Mr. Dalby from Bow Street called earlier and questioned the family and the staff, milord."

"Thank you, Fiske." Jason had expected it after having sent a message to advise the magistrate at Bow Street of his findings, along with the poisoned bottle of tonic.

He entered the drawing room, hoping to find Lady Helen, but Lady Kinsey sat alone.

"Well, what news, Lord Peyton?" she asked. "Bow Street has been most unhelpful."

"I'm afraid I have no news, Lady Kinsey. But I remain undaunted. I hope to interview the rest of the staff today, beginning with the housekeeper, if that is convenient. And I have some questions for his lordship's secretary."

"Of course. But my staff are already most unsettled at having been grilled by Mr. Dalby. He reduced one of the upstairs maids to tears. I know you will deal with them in a more sympathetic manner, but I doubt you'll learn any more than he did."

"One can but hope, my lady."

"Indeed. We must continue until the murderer is found." Lady Kinsey's gray eyes darkened. "I pray the matter is at an end before the ball is held." She clasped her hands tightly in her lap. "How could we invite guests to stay at Kinsey House with a murder hanging over our heads?"

"I do understand your concern," Jason said. "Is there anyone you haven't mentioned? A recent houseguest perhaps?"

"Only Lord Nicholas, Kinsey's younger brother. He stayed with us for a month. But I don't see how he can be of interest to you."

"When did he leave?"

"Several weeks ago."

"Has he remained in London?"

"No. I believe he's in Kent visiting his father, the Marquess, at his country seat, Walcott."

"He was here when Bart fell ill?"

She frowned, reading his thoughts. "Nicholas left here at around that time."

When Lady Kinsey's mouth tightened, Jason sought for a tactful way to ask what he must. Second sons who failed to inherit, or go into the church, the army, or the law, could be short of funds, particularly if a small stipend had to be stretched to accommodate a love of gambling. Lord Nicholas wouldn't be the first of the *beau monde* to commit a crime. Especially if money was involved, and Jason considered it a more likely motive than revenge, although he had too little to go on to be sure of anything. "I'm afraid I must ask these difficult questions, my lady."

"Of course, you must. But Nicholas is a favorite of my children. His nieces and nephews adore him. He's on the verge of marrying. Why he would want to kill our footman is beyond imagining." She sighed. "If that is all, Fiske will escort you to the library and notify Mrs. Chance."

In the library, Jason was exploring more of the fabulous collection when a woman in black came into the room. She had an efficient look about her that seemed to go with housekeepers. Never a hair out of place, and hers, as black as a raven's wing, was neatly swept beneath her cap. She nodded unsmilingly at him. Her strong features might be called handsome, but even when young, she would never have been pretty. He'd seen the lady enter the garden gate with her basket on the day he first met Lord Tobias and Lady Diana.

"Mrs. Chance, milord."

"How do you do. Please be seated, Mrs. Chance."

She sat on the leather sofa and smoothed her skirts with brisk strokes, a chatelaine of keys jingling at her waist. "I fear I shan't be of much use to you."

"You packed up Bart's effects. Can you tell me what you found?"

"Only a few clothes, a book, and his toilette things. His nightclothes were sent to be laundered and used for cleaning cloths. His footman's livery remains with the house."

"I believe you and Bart had a disagreement?"

"He was insolent."

He leaned forward in his chair. "Insolent? How so?"

Her brown eyes grew frosty at the memory. "He refused to run an errand for me."

"What was the errand?"

"It was merely a note for my brother, advising him that I couldn't visit that afternoon. Bart read it, which made me very angry with him."

"How do you know that he read it?"

"Why, he did so in front of me. He was annoyed, said I had no business asking him to deliver personal messages. That he worked for the Kinseys, not me. I planned to go myself, my lord, as my brother expected me, but Lord Nicholas was receiving guests for afternoon tea and we were short staffed. I was needed here." She bristled defensively. "I was forced to caution Bart over the matter."

"Was that the only time you had difficulties?"

"No, as a matter of fact. I took him to task again for lighting a fire in the fireplace in his bedchamber. Fires aren't lit in the staffs' bedchambers, not during the day and certainly not now the weather is warmer."

"And what was his answer?"

"Bart told me to mind my own business, my lord. He got quite above his station. I was planning to speak to Fiske about him, but then Bart became ill." She sighed. "I was sorry then and tried to make him as comfortable as I could."

"Did Bart get on well with the rest of the staff?"

"As far as I know, milord."

"That is all, thank you, Mrs. Chance. Could you please advise the kitchen staff that I wish to speak to them? In about half an hour."

Jason was considering whether to find out which guests Lord Nicholas had entertained when Mr. Thorburn entered.

As he greeted him, Jason was struck again by the man's

pallor. He looked what he was, a veritable bookworm, like those who could be found buried amongst stacks of tomes in libraries.

"I've been hoping to speak to you, my lord." Thorburn sat down at Jason's request, his hands resting on his knees, the picture of earnestness. "I want to help in any way I can."

"You assist Lord Kinsey with his antiquities?"

"Yes. I catalog them, write the necessary correspondence, and sort out where those fascinating finds of his lordship's should go. Some are offered to museums; others his lordship retains. What you see here is just a small part of it. Lord Kinsey has a fine collection at his country estate. And I am expecting a shipment to arrive in London any day from his recent trip." His eyes took on a gleam of anticipation.

"What qualifications does one require for such a position?"

Thorburn straightened his back against the leather squab. "I believe myself eminently qualified. I studied archeology at Cambridge and am able to assist his lordship in deciphering meaning from ancient scripts and languages."

"That must be fascinating work. Do you enjoy it?"

"But of course, my lord. I consider myself very fortunate to have such a position."

Jason rested one leg on his other knee. "Could Bart have had any enemies?"

"I've never seen any evidence of it. I believe he was happy in his employment. Lord Kinsey was quite impressed with him. So much so that he often invited Bart into the library to discuss his work with him."

"Bart was interested in antiquities?" Jason asked, surprised.

"It certainly appeared so. Lord Kinsey even gave him books to read. I often found his lordship and Bart together studying some scroll or other. I wasn't entirely sure that was wise. But my employer is a very generous man. Felt sorry for Bart I imagine. It was a tragedy that Bart lost his arm, but he overcame his disability remarkably well. He appeared to take in every word Lord Kinsey said, I must say."

"Why wouldn't it be wise for Lord Kinsey to divulge his work?" Jason asked, his thoughts returning to the burned letter.

"Some of it should remain confidential."

"And why is that?"

"I'm afraid I cannot say, Lord Peyton. You will have to ask Lord Kinsey."

Jason nodded. "Thank you, Thorburn. If you think of anything, please contact me."

Wishing to ask Fiske if he might be shown down to the servants' hall, Jason left the library. He had not mentioned the burned letter or its contents to Thorburn. He doubted he'd get an answer, even if the man knew what the words electric fish referred to. The secretary appeared intent on guarding Kinsey's secrets. He seemed genuine enough. The son of a wealthy country squire who'd sent his son to university to raise his station in life. But was Thorburn, as he made out, merely a keen student of ancient texts? Happy to remain in Lord Kinsey's shadow? Or might he have bigger aspirations? And what about Bart's aspirations? Jason realized how little he knew about him during the war and nothing about the man he'd become.

Wondering if he'd get a chance to see Helen, Jason rounded a corner and cannoned into a small soft body.

"Lady Helen..." He stepped away and searched her startled flushed face. "I wanted to apologize again for taking such liberties yesterday—"

A flush suffused her creamy cheeks. One glance at her delectable mouth and he remembered the sweet softness and the taste of her, discovering he wanted to repeat the action. It appeared he was a lost cause.

"There's no need, my lord. It was merely the exuberance of the moment and is now forgotten." Averting her eyes, she hurried on. "You are here to discover who killed Bart, and it's my intention to assist you in that aim. Now, who else do you plan to see?"

She sounded so brisk his gaze roamed her serious face, searching for a way to put them both at ease. "The kitchen staff. I believe they're expecting me."

"As Jeremy is out, I shall take you down myself. Please come this way."

She had retreated into the brisk, efficient manner of their first meeting. Regretting that it had been his impulsive act that had caused this change, he had an absurd desire to tease her out of it, wanting to hear her laugh. She cloaked her lively intelligence and sense of humor, but every now and then, he caught an intriguing glimpse. There was no chance of it now, however, as she led him down the servants' stairs. Instead, he told her of his interview with Mrs. Chance.

She shook her head. "That sounds so unlike Bart."

On reaching the servants' hall, Lady Helen introduced

Jason and left him to speak with young Jinx, Cook, and the kitchen and scullery maids, who had gathered together with the gardener and undergardener, shuffling their feet, hats in hand. He soon found everyone to be distressed and nervous, and he came away with nothing useful.

When he returned to the upper floor again, Lady Helen approached him with a hopeful lift of her eyebrows. He shook his head. "Nothing, I'm afraid."

"Bow Street dealt rather harshly with them, poor things," she said. "As if any of them could be responsible for such an act! May I offer you tea, Lord Peyton?"

"I would appreciate it, thank you." He almost grinned at the inquisitive light in her eye. He suspected that her determination to discover Bart's killer overrode her desire to keep him at a distance. He wished perversely that he had something exciting to tell her. "The servants all spoke well of Bart. Said he was one of nature's gentlemen."

"That is true, he was."

"Which makes his rebellious attitude toward Mrs. Chance even more difficult to understand. But she did say she understood he was unwell."

Lady Helen's big eyes grew misty. "Bart would have been in terrible pain. And unable to perform his duties, which would have hurt his pride. He'd achieved so much since the war."

"That's certainly understandable."

In the drawing room, Lady Helen tugged the bell pull. When Fiske appeared, she ordered the tea. "And please ask Cook to add some of her macaroons," she instructed him.

Jason acknowledged her thoughtful gesture with a brief smile.

"Mrs. Chance mentioned that Bart lit a fire in the attic fireplace," Jason said when the footman had left. "Apparently, that isn't permitted except in winter. I gather they were the ashes from the letter fragment we found in the grate."

"I haven't the faintest notion why he would do such a thing. He would never have been deliberately disorderly. And why destroy that letter?" Her eyes glowed with passionate intent. "I do hope we discover who did this!"

"We will," he said emphatically. He wanted to see that passionate light in her eyes for an entirely different reason. Heat flooded through his body, tightening his loins. Shocked, he sat back and crossed his legs. Lady Helen had the unfortunate effect of turning him into an ungainly youth. But there was something heady in the air, even though they both fought the attraction.

"What if Bart didn't burn the letter?" Jason asked, enjoying looking at her, the delicate line of her jaw, and her firm chin, where a dimple appeared when she smiled.

"Oh! I hadn't thought of that." She ran a finger along her plump bottom lip, which hardly helped him gain control of himself. "It isn't so farfetched to believe that Bart wrote the letter to warn someone, the reason for which we are yet to discover, and the person who poisoned him burned it."

Jason smiled into her lovely eyes. "My thoughts exactly."

The heightened atmosphere dissolved when Lady Kinsey entered.

"I believe Lord Nicholas received guests while he was

here?" Jason asked.

Lady Kinsey sat next to her daughter. "It was just before Kinsey departed. Lord and Lady Howard, came with their son, Gareth, and their daughter, Felicity, who is Nicholas' fiancée."

"They were discussing the wedding, which is to be held at St George's next month," Helen added.

"Had they visited before?"

"But of course," Lady Kinsey said, "they are regular dinner guests."

"While Bart was in service?"

"Yes. Both he and Jeremy attended them."

"Did anyone leave the drawing room during that time?"

Helen nodded thoughtfully. "Lady Felicity left with a maid at one point. And my father, Lord Howard, and Gareth spent an hour in the library with their cheroots and brandy."

"Did you notice if anyone spoke to Bart?"

"I couldn't say what occurred in the library, but not here in the drawing room," Helen said.

Lady Kinsey lowered her head, looking defeated. "I can't imagine they'll want to visit us again with this hanging over our heads. But I think you're drawing a long bow there, Peyton."

"You are most likely correct, my lady, but I cannot leave any stone unturned," he said, attempting to hide his frustration.

After a cup of tea and two moreish coconut macaroons, Jason prepared to depart. Seeing Lady Helen again was the highlight of another fruitless search for clues. As the magistrate exhibited no interest in the case, which still could be perceived as an accidental poisoning, he supposed he would now waste the rest of the day at Bow Street.

Hailing a hackney, he sat back and crossed his arms, reflecting on his own surprising behavior. He responded to feminine beauty; he was a man after all. But he couldn't remember a woman affecting him quite the way Lady Helen did. She didn't flirt with him. In fact, she'd made it quite plain the kiss was to be forgotten.

A mocking voice in his head suggested that his regret was merely a blow to his ego. It wasn't. It was something far more profound. He had sensed for some time that Helen carried a wound to her soul, which called to him, perhaps because of his own sad history. He had little confidence this enlightenment would lead them anywhere, however. Not with the strong wall she'd built around herself to keep out the world. But it had become imperative that he earn her trust.

~~~

When her mother became busy with her charity, she asked Helen to discuss the preparations for the ball with Mrs. Chance.

Helen sought out the housekeeper, while her thoughts returned, as they were wont to do, to Peyton. She had been determined to remain cool with him and keep their relationship on a business footing. To forget the soft touch of his lips on hers, and his scent, which was so very masculine. But as soon as he appeared before her so big and familiar, she was lost. The way he smiled at her made her feel as if she was the only woman in the world. Charm, she told herself furiously. That was all it was. Her time must be better spent, discovering what she could to help him, instead of acting like a mooncalf.

Finding herself at Mrs. Chance's parlor door, she took a breath and straightened her shoulders.

The housekeeper was at her desk, her ledger opened before her. "Please don't get up, Mrs. Chance." Helen sat in a wooden chair. "My mother wishes me to ask you if there are any problems remaining to be dealt with before the ball."

"I did wish to consult her ladyship about the curtains in the blue chamber. They are badly faded."

"There's no time to change them now. Might we replace them with those in the unused family chamber? Admittedly they are cream, not blue, and quite plain, but will surely suffice."

"That should do nicely. I shall see it is done. We have sufficient linens for the guest chambers. Some of the towels must be replaced. I thought of ordering a dozen."

"Yes, please do."

Mrs. Chance glanced at her ledger. "The crystal chandelier in the ballroom has been taken down and cleaned. The flowers your mother requested for the urns have been ordered. The window cleaner and the chimney sweep have been in and the carpets in the guest chambers taken up and beaten. Fiske has inspected the cellars and ordered Madeira and French champagne. Cook has the menu for the supper dishes."

"You seem to have it well in hand, Mrs. Chance. Mother has every faith in you."

"Thank you, Lady Helen."

"I have another matter to discuss with you."

Mrs. Chance pushed her ledger away. "Yes?"

"It concerns your quarrel with Bart."

The housekeeper's dark brows rose sharply. "It was more a slight disagreement than a quarrel."

"I have difficulty equating his behavior with the Bart I knew."

"I thought the same at the time." Mrs. Chance sighed heavily. "I realized afterward that he was defensive because he couldn't do his work."

"I sent Bart on several errands the week before he took to his bed. He seemed to manage well."

The housekeeper nodded. "He would do his best for the family, poor fellow."

"Why did he say to you, *you must think me a fool*?"

Mrs. Chance blinked. "I don't recall Bart saying any such thing."

"He was overheard by one of the staff."

"Was it one of the maids? She must have misunderstood."

"They seemed quite certain."

"My goodness what nonsense. If it was Eloise, her English is not very reliable."

When Helen didn't answer, she gave a bemused shake of her head. "Bart would have no reason to say it. I wouldn't treat him in such a cavalier fashion. He was no fool, as you know, Lady Helen. I was cross with him at the time, but as soon as I realized what lay behind it, I deeply regretted my attitude. No one should suffer the way he did. I felt for him and tried my best to make him comfortable."

"Yes, I know you did, Mrs. Chance, for which we are most grateful." Helen studied the housekeeper's stony countenance. She had never seen her as the motherly sort.

"Whoever said such a thing must have misheard." She frowned. "Or lied. Alice causes nothing but trouble. She'd set her cap at Bart and knew I disapproved. Bart flirted with her, but he also favored Eloise. I could foresee trouble ahead if it was allowed to continue."

"Very sensible, Mrs. Chance." Helen stood. "Thank you for explaining the situation. And please come to me, if there's anything else."

Helen located Alice in one of the guest bedchambers on her knees cleaning the grate. She clambered to her feet and wiped a sooty hand over her cheek, her honey-colored curls peeping from her cap. "You wished to see me, milady?"

A pretty, fresh-faced country girl of eighteen, when Alice had first been employed at Cherrywood before coming to Kinsey House, Helen had feared she'd be homesick for the country, but she seemed happy here. "I have a question, Alice. You won't get into any trouble, I promise you, but please answer me honestly."

She clutched the cleaning cloth in nervous fingers. "Yes, milady?"

"Was there anything more than friendship between you and Bart?"

Her blue eyes filled with tears. "Yes, milady. We hoped to marry one day."

"Mrs. Chance disapproved?"

Alice nibbled her lower lip. "She did. She said it wasn't

done for staff to marry each other, and if that was the case, I should seek other employment."

"What did Bart say to that?"

"He was angry. Said she had no such authority. He planned to have a word with you. But then he got sick." She flushed. "I don't have to leave now, do I, Lady Helen? I like working here, and me ma would be so upset."

"No, of course not, Alice. You can visit with your family when we return to Cherrywood in October."

"Me ma will be so pleased to see me, Lady Helen."

"I'm sure she will. And I'm sorry, I wasn't aware that you and Bart planned to marry. You must miss him dreadfully. But are you absolutely sure you heard correctly when he accused Mrs. Chance of thinking him a fool?"

Alice sniffed and wiped her eyes with the corner of her apron. "I did, Lady Helen. Clear as day."

Helen's first thought as she left the room was to tell Peyton about the latest information she'd gleaned when next he called. How hopeless she'd become! She sighed, vexed with herself, and hurried to her bedroom to change her gown. She was to accompany Diana on a shopping jaunt to purchase bonnets and fripperies, and for once, Helen welcomed the distraction, desperate to banish the handsome man from her mind. She must not allow herself to consider the impossible, that she might find happiness, for that was rare, elusive, and, in her experience, fleeting.

CHAPTER TWELVE

In the Bow Street magistrate's house, Jason learned that the magistrate's findings declared Bart's death a probable suicide because he was already desperately ill and in great pain. Dalby, the Bow Street runner, had lost interest in the case.

"It's like finding a needle in a stack of hay," he said. "Can't afford to waste me time on it when there's ready money to be made elsewhere."

"I thought Lady Kinsey employed you," Jason said, surprised but also relieved to have free rein to find the killer. Runners always looked for a lucrative job. Surely this was one.

Dalby's expression turned sour. "Fired me. Said she'd rather you dealt with it, milord. Feels it's a delicate matter. Doesn't want me upsetting the household."

"Did you turn up anything?"

"A long shot, but it's possible the tonic was tampered with before it reached Kinsey House. Bartholomew Smythe was known to enjoy a few ales at the Lamb and Flag in

Westminster on his afternoons off. The innkeeper recalls him showing the bottle to the drinkers in the taproom."

Jason took a hackney to the narrow brick two-story inn situated in Lazenby Court, a back lane off Rose Street, known for its bare-knuckle fighting.

In the lane outside the pub, two lady-birds in their shabby finery sidled up to Jason with hopeful smiles. He winked, shook his head, and entered the taproom. A blend of unpleasant odors greeted him in the damp air, hops, smoke, and unwashed bodies. Jason wondered what the attraction such a place had for Bart. Perhaps just the fellowship he'd enjoyed in the army. A lone sailor sat in a corner, staring forlornly into his ale.

"Bart was in high dudgeon that evening, milord. Eager to draw someone's cork," the innkeeper said, running a cloth over the tables. His broken nose, muscled chest, and tattooed, beefy forearms revealed a history of bare-knuckle boxing and time spent in the Navy. "Picked an argument with some cove."

"What did the man look like?"

"Eh? Big dark-haired bruiser. Not one of me regulars. I had to separate the two of 'em in the end." He shook his head and chuckled. "Pluck to the backbone was Bart. Wanted to prove he could win a fight with one arm. He accounted for himself well with an excellent right hook. Drew quite an audience. But while they was sorting it out, he'd left his tonic bottle on the table, and it got knocked over. Didn't spill, but anyone could have got at it with everyone watching the fight."

Jason shook his head. "Hardly likely to carry arsenic around on them."

"But they wouldn't have to, milord. I keep it here." He gestured with his thumb at the cupboard door behind him. "Use it to get rid of the rats. It's common knowledge."

"Do you think any of them were likely to do Bart in with arsenic?"

He paused then shook his head. "They'd prefer using their fists or knives to poison. Poisoning's a woman's game."

Jason nodded toward the door into the inn's parlor, where the two women sat drinking. "Did Bart show any interest in the light-skirts?"

"Saw 'em approach him a few times, but Bart didn't seem to be in the petticoat line."

Jason took out some coins and placed them on the table. "Would you ask your regulars who witnessed Bart's fight if they know what caused it? I'll be back in a day or so."

The innkeeper's words stayed with Jason as he traveled home. He'd heard the view expressed that women favored poison. But he was sure Newgate had accommodated its fair share of male poisoners in the cells. Could Bart have come to grief at the hands of someone in the Lamb and Flag? As Dalby had suggested, it did seem to be a long shot.

Jason's mood didn't improve after he'd walked through the door. It seemed both his siblings were unhappy, although only one was unhappy with him, at least.

"You were to escort me to the art gallery today, Jas." Lizzie glared at him as they drank a glass of wine before dinner. "But you had left when I came down to breakfast and have been gone all day."

He'd become so caught up with finding Bart's killer that

he'd clean forgotten today was the day he'd promised to go to the exhibition. Unlike him to break a promise. He grimaced. It made him realize how involved he'd become with this investigation. "Lord, I'm sorry, Lizzie. Will tomorrow do?"

"I suppose it will, but the Baron did appear downcast by your indifference."

"It wasn't indifference. I've been caught up in something that demands my attention. A family in need, Lizzie."

"The Kinseys, I know."

Jason gave a bark of laughter. "How do you know?"

"I heard you giving directions to a hackney driver from my window, yesterday. So, unless it's one of the Kinsey girls you wish to see, I gather it was business."

He shook his head with a grin. "I'll apologize to the baron. Though I don't think my attendance would matter too much."

"Oh, but it does. He often speaks of you."

Jason raised his eyebrows. "Does he?"

"Yes, he's always asking about you."

"Asking what exactly?"

"Nothing in particular. You had told him you'd been to Italy, and he wished to know more about that. But I don't know much about your trip, something to do with the government, wasn't it? I was enjoying being married. Greywood was home on leave. I told the baron that you distinguished yourself under Wellington during the war."

"How very dull for the poor fellow." It occurred to him that Bianchi might be about to offer for Lizzie's hand. The prospect didn't please him as much as he'd hoped. "Does the exhibition go well?"

A faint line creased her brow. "I need to speak to you about that."

The door opened, and Charlie stalked into the drawing room.

"After dinner," Lizzie added.

Jason looked uneasily at her. "Very well." He turned to eye his brother, who was scowling. "Good evening, Charlie."

"I can't see much that's good about it." Charlie took a glass of wine from Henry. "I only have a few weeks left before I must return to Oxford."

"I thought you'd come to terms with going back." Jason nodded his thanks to Fiske, who'd just decanted a fresh bottle of claret.

"I suppose I have, but I hoped to secure Amelia's affections before I left."

Jason took a good mouthful of wine, savoring the taste of black cherry, licorice, and spice before hearing the worst. "Not going well?"

"A fellow with a face like a trout escorted Amelia to the theater. And when I questioned her about it, she insisted that she's free to go out with whomever she pleases."

"But, Charlie, Miss Groton is quite correct," Lizzie said gently. "You have no claim on her."

"That's because she keeps me at arm's length." A deep breath pushed out his chest. "Can't understand it. Girls have shown a partiality for me in the past."

"I'm sure they still do," Lizzie said with a sympathetic smile. "But it's possible this other man has more to offer.

After all, you'll be at university for another year, and after that, you're to make your grand tour. You can't expect Miss Groton to wait so long for you."

Charlie shook his head. "I've decided not to take the tour."

"What? Have you thought it through, Charlie?" Jason was worried that his brother's infatuation might cause him to make hasty decisions. "I had the best time of my life touring the Continent with a group of lads."

A spark appeared in Charlie's green eyes. "Wasn't it a total bore, Jas?"

"*Au contraire!* Wine, women, and song." Jason grinned. "Beg pardon, Lizzie."

"That is not what the tour is meant to be about, Charlie. It is designed to turn you into a cultured gentleman." Lizzie frowned at Jason and firmed her lips, but Jason didn't miss the laughter in her eyes before she lowered her head over her wine glass.

After dinner, when Charlie had gone to meet a friend for a game of billiards, Jason and Lizzie settled in the library. He poured a glass of Madeira for her and port for himself. "What worries you so, Lizzie? Does it concern the baron?"

"Someone has accused him of selling a forged artwork."

"Really? One in his collection? I wasn't aware he intended to sell any of them."

She traced a drop of condensation down her glass. "Neither was I, but it turns out that he does buy and sell paintings."

"Which piece of work is it?"

"Come tomorrow and ask him. I believe it's a drawing by Albrecht Dürer. The man is to bring it to the gallery."

"Yes, of course. I'm no expert, but I'll be interested to see it."

Bianchi was entitled to buy and sell his paintings if he wished. What bothered Jason was the fact that the baron had misled him. He'd said it was his love of sharing his art collection with the world that had brought him to London. Might he be involved in fraud? Tomorrow he would take a closer look at the baron's dealings.

~~~

Helen and Diana had spent several delightful hours shopping at Thomas's Fashionable Warehouse at the West End corner of Chancery Row, near Temple-Bar, buying ribbons and hosiery, shawls, and fans. At Marchant & Co, in New Bond Street, with their wonderful display of leghorn hats, straw chips, and all manner of bonnets, Diana tried on a dark straw with a huge ostrich feather that dipped over her face. She posed before the mirror. "This is the latest thing. What do you think?"

Helen considered it far too old for her. "Too fussy. Simpler styles suit you best. I do like that gray-blue silk with the camellias around the brim for myself."

Diana removed the hat and handed it to the saleswoman. "You're right, Helen. Thank you, Miss Brown. "I'll try that wide-brimmed straw."

As the saleswoman went to fetch both hats, Diana turned from the mirror. "I believe Lord Peyton visited us again yesterday while I was in the music room with Master Benne."

"Yes. Peyton is still searching for a reason for Bart's death."

Diana's blue eyes clouded. "But why?"

Helen took a deep breath. "Peyton hasn't discounted the possibility that Bart might have been deliberately poisoned." As the investigation dragged on, she'd come to realize it was inevitable Diana would find out and, despite her mother's warning, believed her sister had a right to know.

Diana gasped. "It wasn't an accident?"

"Lord Peyton is unsure what occurred. But he will find out, have no fear."

"But if Bart was deliberately poisoned, then the poisoner might still be amongst us." She put a fist to her mouth. "Oh, how dreadful!"

Helen placed a hand on Diana's shoulder. "The tonic might have been tampered with before Bart brought it home. We can't be sure what the herbalist put in it."

Diana sagged in the seat. "Yes, that seems far more likely. I can't imagine anyone in Kinsey House would do such a thing."

"I have every confidence in Peyton discovering the answer."

Helen watched the saleswoman arrange the straw embellished with blue silk flowers and ribbons around the crown on Diana's head. "My, that hat does suit you!"

"Yes, I do like it." Diana turned her head from side to side.

Helen eased out a breath. As Diana's ball grew closer, she did not want her sister caught up in the possibility of murder. But Diana was perceptive and intelligent. It would be hard to keep things from her.

Diana adjusted the hat. "What do you think of Lord Peyton? You've seen quite a lot of him of late."

Diana's casual inquiry didn't fool Helen. No doubt her sister planned to dazzle the earl at the ball. "He seems a decent man."

"Yes, that was my impression. Mama says he's accepted the invitation, along with his sister and younger brother. I hope to dance with Peyton. Dancing with a man must tell you so much about him, don't you think?"

"I imagine so." Helen allowed herself a brief vision of the handsome earl, his arms around her guiding her over the ballroom floor as Miss Brown placed the gray-blue silk with the camellias on her head. "No, I don't care for this. It's a little drab," Helen said.

"And much too old for you," Diana observed.

"Dancing must be a little like making love." Diana leaned forward to closely examine the stitching that held the blue flowers in place. "Mama said that after she danced with Papa she made up her mind to marry him."

Miss Brown hovered with an emerald green poke bonnet in her hands, and her mouth dropped open.

"Hush." Helen recalled her own horrible experiences at the hands of nasty gossips. "You would not want anyone to think you fast, Diana, before you've even stepped out into Society." She glanced at Miss Brown, obviously bursting to relate the tale to the owner of the establishment. "I know we feel we can be quite comfortable here and can rely on the discretion of Madam Marchant and her staff. Is that not so, Miss Brown?"

"Oh, indeed it is," Miss Brown said with a bob.

Helen smiled. "I believe we'll take that lovely straw. And I do like that emerald green velvet. It will match my new pelisse perfectly. How very clever of you to bring it."

Helen nodded her approval as Miss Brown arranged the bonnet over her hair. Diana's interest in Peyton had not waned. Her sister was so vibrant and full of life. What man could resist her?

When they reached home laden with packages, the hatboxes piled up in Jeremy's arms, Mama greeted them in the hall. She waved a letter. "Your father is delayed once again," she said in a vexed tone. "Business has kept him in Liverpool. Some shipment has gone missing. But a consignment from Egypt arrived this morning. Mr. Thorburn is dealing with it in the library."

"But Papa will be here in time for my ball?" Diana cried.

"As if your papa would miss that!" Mama wrapped an arm around Diana's waist and led her into the morning room. She sat with her on the sofa while Jeremy brought in their shopping. "Show me what you've bought."

Helen slipped away intent on going to the library while Mama and Diana examined their purchases and discussed fashion. Plato ambushed her in the corridor, and she swept him up. Mr. Thorburn, his face flushed, was on his hands and knees on the library floor as she entered, pulling straw out of several big boxes. Intriguing artifacts and other pieces unfathomable to her unpracticed eye lay on the carpet around him.

He looked up and blinked behind his glasses. "Oh, Lady Helen. Such things your father has sent home! They fair take my breath away!"

"Can I be of help, Mr. Thorburn?" As fascinated as he, Helen put the cat down. She yearned to travel to Eastern climes with her father and discover such things for herself. But Papa would never consider taking her. Not since the ball. She was bitterly aware that he viewed her as too nervous for such a venture. Even though it was no longer true. She had regained her strength and could tackle anything that came her way and could only hope that, in time, she could change his mind.

"I should be most grateful if you could help me to group them for cataloging," Mr. Thorburn said. "Just a preliminary list at this stage, you understand."

"I shall be pleased to." Helen sat behind the desk. As she selected pen and paper, she noticed a letter from Alexandro Volta at the top of the pile awaiting her father's perusal. "Is Mr. Volta a friend of my father's?"

Mr. Thorburn's head whipped up, his features tight. He rose and came to the desk. "I don't believe so. I meant to put that letter away."

She watched as he took the letter and slipped it inside a leather-bound portfolio.

His shoulders relaxed, and he smiled as he returned to kneel beside the wooden crate. "Now, shall we begin?"

He began to pull out straw, murmuring with delight over the objects he found within the crate. He carefully placed a granite statue of a proudly erect cat on the floor beside him. "Bastet, protectress of cats. The Ancient Egyptians had great respect for the animals," he murmured. "Killing a cat was punishable by death."

"That should be an English law, too."

He looked up and grinned. "Cats protected the grain from mice and rats. If a cat died, the family would mourn it by shaving their eyebrows."

"I'm sure you would agree, wouldn't you, Plato?" she asked the cat, who was flicking a piece of straw about with its paws.

She turned her attention back to Thorburn, hunched over the box. Why didn't he wish her to see Volta's letter? Might he be hiding something? Or did he think that she, as a woman, should not involve herself too deeply in her father's work? She dabbed the pen in the inkwell and began to list the items when the secretary named them. But her pulse still raced. Perhaps the secrets she and Peyton sought resided in that portfolio. As soon as the secretary left the library, she would return.

When Thorburn left the house, Helen continued her examination of the portfolio. She was so intent on its contents she didn't hear the door open, only sensed that someone had stepped into the room.

"Oh, I beg your pardon, Lady Helen. I thought the library was empty. One of the maids has lost her workbox. I'm sure she'd forget her head if it wasn't attached to her neck."

"I haven't seen it here, Mrs. Chance, but please look around."

The housekeeper's gaze swept around the room. "No, not here."

When the door closed again, Helen returned to the fascinating contents of the portfolio.

CHAPTER THIRTEEN

At the Mayfair art gallery, Baron Bianchi appeared eager to gain Jason's support. "I sell very few paintings from my collection, although I donate some to art galleries. But this patron was so keen I didn't wish to disappoint him, and the drawing was not a particular favorite of mine." He shook his head. "I should have sensed something was wrong. Now I must be on my guard, Lord Peyton. I fear I've been the subject of a hoax."

"Your buyer is returning with the drawing today?"

"I expect him any moment. It distresses me that you must witness it."

"I'm afraid I can't be of much help to you. I certainly can't offer you a critical opinion."

The baron placed a hand on Jason's arm. "But that was never my intention, Lord Peyton! As you will soon observe, I have sought expert advice." He shrugged and rolled his dark eyes. Smiling warmly at Lizzie, he placed his arm at her back to lead her forward. "I am like an eager youth wishing for you to see my art collection. Please take your brother around the room, Lady Greywood." He waved his hand. "Your opinion is keenly sought. Do you feel I have displayed my paintings to advantage?"

Jason had already circled the room once with Lizzie and was about to do so again. He glanced at the impressive works of art. Several of the paintings were breathtaking and worth a good deal of money. "A magnificent collection, Baron."

The hairs on the back of his neck only stirred when something, yet to reveal itself, disturbed him. Perhaps it was the baron's overly familiar manner toward Lizzie. They were not betrothed. The way that he guided Lizzie around with a hand at her waist was not acceptable behavior in England. But perhaps the baron did not know that. Jason was aware that Italian culture was different.

He examined the reason for his strong dislike. Was he being unreasonable? Or just resistant to the idea of Bianchi snatching his sister away from England? He turned to study Bianchi, who was laughingly rearranging Lizzie's shawl. She would not marry him until he was quite sure the man was sound.

A slight, nervous fellow entered the gallery with a package wrapped in brown paper and tied with string tucked under his arm. He hurried over to them. "Baron Bianchi, I have brought the drawing." Breathing heavily, he began to tug at the strings.

Bianchi put out a hand to prevent him. "My expert, Mr. Barrett, has not yet arrived, Mr. Gillies. Please allow me to introduce my good friend, Lord Peyton. His sister, Lady Greywood, you met yesterday. Do look around the room at your leisure, and we shall discuss this matter when Mr. Barrett arrives."

As Gillies wandered reluctantly away, Bianchi turned to Jason, his dark eyes hard as granite. "This is an embarrassment for which I must apologize. I did not wish to involve you, Lord Peyton. But I shall have to deal with it. I have engaged a table for luncheon at the hotel across the street and should be delighted if you would join me there."

Jason accepted, determined to learn more.

"I won't keep you now. Please go, enjoy a glass of wine, and I will join you as soon as I have finished. The work is genuine. It will take but a moment to establish the fact."

Jason took Lizzie's arm. She resisted as he guided her toward the door, but he firmly drew her out into the street.

She glared at him. "I want to see what occurs."

"Lord Bianchi will tell us in his own time. Be patient, Lizzie."

A waiter led them to a table near the window, and Jason ordered wine. Across the street, a dark-haired man entered the gallery, carrying a valise. Through the long windows, he saw Bianchi welcoming him and introducing him to Mr. Gillies.

"What's happening?" Lizzie frowned, her view obscured by a pillar.

"They have gone into another room," Jason said. "Sherry?"

Lizzie looked pale, her large eyes strained. "Thank you, I feel the need of one."

Jason signaled the waiter. His sister wasn't lacking in

perception. Had she begun to suspect Bianchi was not quite what he appeared? Questions filled his mind. Why had the baron wanted him here? Was it merely to lend him some measure of credibility? Who was this so-called expert he'd called in? Jason would question Bianchi more closely than perhaps the baron would like when he joined them for luncheon.

He opened the menu. "Scalloped oysters or some cold chicken?"

"I couldn't eat a bite." Lizzie pleated the linen napkin in her fingers.

"You aren't committed to this man, Lizzie," Jason said carefully. "If you've changed your mind about him, you have only to say."

Her worried green eyes met his. "I was happy with him, Jas. Life in England has been trying since Greywood died. I see a future for myself with him."

Widowhood could be hard on women. He could almost hear Helen observing how men could marry again immediately, but women were isolated from society and forced to dress in drab clothing. With a pang, he patted Lizzie's hand. "You're assured of an excellent future without him in it. There are many men, dozens," he added with a wink, "eager to make you happy, should you let them."

She sighed. "At my age, a widower with children, I suppose. English peers only wed when they have to and seldom to someone my age."

"That's true of some, but not all."

"Oh? Look at you, almost thirty-three and still not married." She leaned forward. "And with no intention of it. Oh, but you feel the Peyton line is secure with Charlie, don't you?"

No intention of it? Jason turned his wine glass in his fingers, watching it catch the light. "Yes, it is. But I wouldn't say that I never intend to tie the knot."

Lizzie's eyes brightened. "It's one of the Kinsey girls. I knew it as soon as I received an invitation to Lady Diana's ball. I've heard she's a beauty."

Jason was saved from answering by Bianchi, who came bustling through the door. All smiles, he greeted them formally and took a seat at the table. "The matter is at an end. Utter nonsense! Mr. Barrett soon confirmed the drawing was genuine."

"That is excellent news," Lizzie said gaily.

Jason echoed her response, in a soberer tone, and glanced through the window to where Mr. Gillies scurried away, head down, clutching his package. He did not appear to be happy to discover his drawing was genuine. Jason decided to write again to Vale in Florence.

"Shall we order champagne?" Bianchi smiled and patted Lizzie's hand. "I believe it's called for in the circumstances."

"I'll stick to wine thank you," Jason said. "Tell me, Baron, are you confident that Mr. Barrett has the right qualifications to make such a judgment? Art forgeries are sometimes extremely difficult to detect. Especially Dürer, who has been copied many times since the sixteenth century."

"The woodcuts certainly. But there is no doubt this drawing was done by the artist on blue paper." Bianchi's smile dimmed, and he turned to signal the waiter. "I have complete faith in Mr. Barrett. I've consulted him on several occasions."

"Where did you purchase the drawing?"

"From a respected gallery in Venice. That city is where Dürer lived for a time." Bianchi picked up his napkin and lowered his head as he settled the linen over his lap. "I have shown the receipt of my purchase to both Mr. Barrett and Mr. Gillies." He smiled at Lizzie. "The oysters are always very fresh here, Lady Greywood. I wonder if you can be tempted?"

As Lizzie demurred, Jason wondered why Bianchi employed an Englishman. Why not an expert from Italy or France or even Germany? He had not exhibited his art in London before. While he drank his wine, he decided to locate Mr. Gillies and check the credentials of this Mr. Barrett, to ensure all was as the baron said. The matter had been resolved too hastily for his liking. Shouldn't the drawing be studied with more care? And compared with Dürer's other works?

"I'm afraid I must leave you directly after luncheon," he said, aware that he would not be missed because Lizzie and the baron were now sharing a private smile. He would return to the Lamb and Flag and call again at the Kinsey's afterward, hopefully with news.

~~~

After Mr. Thorburn had left the house, Helen slipped into the library. She opened the portfolio and sat down to read through the pile of letters, drawings, and her father's notes. She could understand little of the correspondence from Mr. Volta, as the man's hand was a scrawl and Italian was not one of the languages in which she was proficient. What she did discern made her cheeks flush with excitement. She couldn't wait to show this to Peyton.

A knock at the door made her hastily return the letters to the portfolio. She was inspecting one of the new additions to her father's collection when Mrs. Chance came in.

"Yes, Mrs. Chance?"

"Milady, we will be short one housemaid for the weekend of the ball."

"Oh? Who have we lost, Mrs. Chance? And why?"

"It's Alice. She is unwell."

"I'm sorry to hear that. What seems to be the matter?"

"A stomach complaint. Fiske plans to ask your mother when she comes home if Mr. Belvedere can be called. But Alice may have recovered by tomorrow."

Helen's chest tightened. "Has anyone else been ill?"

"No. It seems an isolated case."

Helen jumped up. "I'll go and see her."

"Should another maid be employed in the interim, milady? I would ask Lady Kinsey, but she's been away all day, and with the ball approaching…"

"An excellent idea. Send Jeremy to the employment agency please, Mrs. Chance. It's short notice, but please try anyway."

Helen hurried up to Alice's room. She found the maid hunched over in her bed, her face startlingly pale.

"What is the matter, Alice?" she asked with another lurch of fear.

"I don't know what it can be, Lady Helen. I haven't felt

myself for a week, but the pains are worse today."

"Do you think you might have eaten something that upset you?"

"No. Just the regular meals Cook serves us."

Helen sat on the bed. "We'll have you well in no time. The doctor will be here soon."

"Oh, milady! I can't have him looking at me stomach. It's not proper."

"I shall ensure another woman is present in the room, Alice. Mr. Belvedere is an experienced and discreet doctor and will behave in a perfectly correct manner."

A spasm of pain crossed her face. "If you're sure, Lady Helen."

Helen squeezed Alice's hand. "I am. The doctor will give you something to make you feel better. You'll be right as rain in no time."

Alice lay back weakly. "I do hope so. With the ball in a week and guests coming to stay. Who will do me work?"

"That has already been taken care of. You are not to worry about the ball, Alice. Just rest."

Helen left the attic room eager for her mother to return. A chill washed over her. She needed her father. But even more, although she had no right to wish it, she needed Peyton, his strength, his warmth, his reassuring smile.

CHAPTER FOURTEEN

Jason had no trouble locating Mr. Gillies. The small thin gentleman lived in a respectable part of town. He stood for a moment on the street wondering why he was pursuing the matter. Did he suspect Bianchi was guilty of fraud, or did he just wish him to be? He had to admit that his feelings for the Baron were decidedly antipathetic.

"I was left some money by a relative," Mr. Gillies explained over a glass of wine and biscuits in his sitting room. "It is my long-held dream to fill my house with beautiful art. This is my first purchase." He nodded toward the framed sketch of a pair of male hands pressed together in prayer on blue paper, purported to be by Dürer, where it hung in pride of place on the wall. If it was a copy, it was very well done.

"When did you purchase this from Baron Bianchi?" Jason asked.

"About two months ago here in London."

Jason took a sip of wine, finding it a good vintage.

"What made you suspect the work is a forgery?"

"A friend of mine who is a collector has seen what he believes to be the original in a gallery in Vienna."

"Perhaps this is that drawing?"

Gillies shook his head. "My friend has only just returned."

"Then is it possible, perhaps, that the one your friend saw is a forgery?"

Gillies jaw sagged. "Impossible to say."

"So the expert has assured you the Dürer is authentic? Do you know much about Barrett?"

"Nothing. His card states he is connected to the esteemed establishment, The Royal Academy of Arts."

"But you still seem unsure, Mr. Gillies?"

Gillies sat up straighter. "I remain unconvinced. Do you know of someone who might help?"

"I would advise consulting Mr. John Smith in New Bond Street. He is undoubtedly the best in the business. I have written to a friend in Florence who knows Bianchi and has viewed his collection. I'm not sure what might result from it if anything."

"I am most grateful. I shall certainly consult Mr. Smith." He hesitated. "There is something else."

"Yes?"

"Might be nothing. Barrett purports to be English, in conversation he mentioned he hails from York. He's no Yorkshireman. He's no Englishman, in fact."

"What makes you so sure?"

"A swarthy fellow, but that's by the by. I served in the army on the Continent in a clerical capacity. I expect my ear is now tuned to languages, for I detected a foreign inflection beneath Barrett's precise English."

"Interesting." Jason finished his wine and stood. "I'll advise you of anything I discover."

Gillies shook his hand. "I am most grateful to you, my lord."

At the Lamb and Flag, the taproom, which smelled of beer and onions, was surprisingly empty of customers. The publican wiping down the oily tables hailed Jason as he walked through the door. "Good day to you, sir. Can I get you an ale?"

"No, thank you. Have you any information for me?"

"I asked around. As I said, most were watching the fight. It's not every day you see a one-armed man handle himself so well."

"True." Jason tried to hide his impatience. "Nothing then?"

"I'm told the fellow who picked a fight with Bart had jeered at him, called him a cripple."

"Deliberately provoked him?"

"Could have. Bart was spoiling for it, though, as I've said." The publican held up a plate-sized hand. "One of my regulars saw another man pick up Bart's bottle. He couldn't see what he did with it, as his back was to him. Might have just read the label for all we know."

"Did you get a description of him?"

He shook his head. "Better dressed than most and short, with dark hair, is all. Haven't seen him in here since."

Jason dropped some coins into the publican's palm then handed him his card. "You've been helpful. The man might turn up again. Anything you feel I should know, send a note to this address. I'll make it worth your while."

The publican grinned. "Bit of skullduggery brightens me life."

As he made his way to Kinsey House, Jason admitted he was far too eager to see Helen again.

Helen, her cheeks flushed, hurried to greet him as Fiske admitted him to the house. "I am pleased that you called, Lord Peyton. Mother isn't here, I'm afraid." She turned to the butler. "We'll have tea in the library, thank you, Fiske."

As soon as the door closed, she turned to him, her gray eyes anguished. "Our housemaid Alice is ill. A painful stomach complaint."

He rubbed his neck as prickles climbed his spine. "The doctor has been called?"

"Yes, but he couldn't discover the cause. As Alice was feeling a little better this morning, we have sent her home to her mother."

Although Helen did not express her fears in so many words, it was clear that the possibility of Alice being poisoned had occurred to her as it had him.

"A wise decision. It's to be hoped she recovers quickly."

"Indeed yes. Alice's mother resides in Cherrywood Village, where there's an excellent doctor should Alice need further treatment. But I have something else to tell you. Yesterday, I noticed a letter from Mr. Volta lying on the desk. When I tried to read it, Mr. Thorburn acted quite oddly. He practically snatched it away from me. After he went home, I returned to read it."

Her concern and vulnerability called to him, but he kept

his hands resolutely at his sides while his desire to take her in his arms warred with his responsibility to shake some sense into her. Alice's illness already had ice threading through his veins. "Prevented you? Not forcefully?"

She walked over to her father's desk. "Now you are teasing me. Of course not. He merely took the letter from me and placed it in this portfolio."

"Why did you attempt to read Volta's letter? Hadn't we decided to wait for your father? You have signaled your interest to Thorburn," he said brusquely. "You might have thought it through. Such an action was rash and could be dangerous."

She turned away from him, her shoulders stiff with indignation. "Why do men think we women incapable of rational thought? Jeremy was outside in the corridor. I knew I was in no danger from Mr. Thorburn."

"You knew no such thing. You thought the risk worth taking."

She waved that away. "If you'll just stop lecturing me, I'll tell you the rest of it. What I have since learned." She selected a leather-covered folder from the desk. "It's all in here. My father's drawings, his discussions with Volta. But I can only read a smattering of Italian. I hoped you can do better." She untied the ribbons and opened it out on the desk.

Still determined to get his point across, he raised an eyebrow at her then sifted through the correspondence, notes, and drawings, pausing to study a sketch taken from the wall of an Egyptian tomb. "I wonder what this is."

She moved closer, drawing his attention away from the etching with the sound of her breath and her womanly scent. Fear for her when he was not here to safeguard her mingled with an increasing desire to grow closer.

"Where is Lady Kinsey?"

"Away from home. Mama's latest charity for poor relief is taking up much of her time." She glowered at him and traced a finger over the sketch. "But is this not extraordinary? These two long glass cylinders the two figures are holding are attached by some length of cord. Inside them looks to be something akin to a pair of electric eels. Of course, I can't decipher the inscription. But I don't doubt my father has done so." Her eyes sought his with an urgency that made him catch his breath. "It appears that Papa and Mr. Volta, who, as we know invented the Voltaic pile, have been working together." She selected a letter. "It says here that they believe this proves that light can be produced from a new and different source, an electrical current of some kind that can light up a lamp and possibly the streets of London."

"Remarkable," he murmured.

"Isn't it?" She leaned over him to sort through the portfolio. "My father has stated in his notes that, when the first foray into Egyptian tombs was made, no sign of candlewax or oil was found to show how the Egyptians lighted those windowless stone spaces. He believes they had discovered another way of producing light and that this drawing, which he translates to mean electric fish, gives a hint of it."

"Good Lord!"

"Yes. I believe Bart was caught up in this."

"That's certainly possible."

Her fingers clutched his sleeve. "Don't you see? Bart must have discovered the plot to steal Papa's plans and was killed for it. Why else turn to the government for help? And another letter from Volta has arrived today."

It was also possible that Bart had been involved initially and then, for some reason, turned against the conspirators. He didn't want to think badly of a man he liked. He reluctantly drew his gaze from Helen's vivid face to study Volta's latest letter. "First, let me see what Volta has to say."

"Yes." She handed him the letter and gestured to the sofa. "Please do."

"I've learned more about Volta, his experiments in electrochemistry," Jason said, sitting down. "The Italian took his findings to Napoleon, who was most impressed. No doubt the French are keen to learn more."

She sat beside him. "I'm afraid Volta's writing and the Italian language defeated me."

The ticking of the ormolu clock on the overmantel filled the quiet room. He was conscious of the impatient lady beside him as he read. When he put the letter down, he knew she would not like what he had to tell her. "Volta writes that he's given the matter much thought but does not wish to pursue it any further."

Tilting her chin down, she frowned at her hands in her lap. "That's definite?"

"I'm afraid so. Volta has retired, and while there's a good deal of promise in what he and your father have discovered, and he does not discount further experiments will lead to producing an alternative to gas, it will be many years before it can be expanded and developed. Especially as gas will soon provide light for all of London."

She twined her fingers together as he watched her excitement ebb away. "Then it has all come to nothing."

"It appears so." He hated to see her disillusioned, but this might stop her searching for answers, and Jason's main concern right now was to keep her safe. "Your father will be disappointed."

"Papa will remain undaunted. I expect his excursions to uncover ancient artifacts will continue. And who knows, he might find more evidence to support his theory and work with another scientist." She sighed.

He averted his gaze from her bosom. "You're disappointed too."

"I had hoped to persuade my father to take me with him on his travels. Mama dislikes the heat too much to accompany him."

Jason found the idea of Lady Helen disappearing off to the East distinctly unpalatable. "He has refused you?"

She shook her head. "I've never asked him, but he would not consider it now."

He wondered what had happened for her to believe this. Before he could ask, Jeremy brought in the tea tray then left.

"So, where to next?" She poured the tea into cups.

Jason told her what he'd discovered at the Lamb and Flag. "I'm not hopeful it will lead us anywhere."

"If Bart's murder was because of this theory concerning electric fish, whoever is involved will surely give up now that Volta has dropped the experiments."

"They would not have learned of it. Even with Volta out

of the picture, your father's discovery will prove to be of immense value to someone. They'll be hoping for more to come."

"And if we keep watch, we can catch them," Helen said, her hand holding a cup paused halfway to her lips.

"*We* are not going to keep watch, Lady Helen," he said sternly. "Please don't raise the subject with Mr. Thorburn again. I'm yet to be convinced he's not involved in this."

She shrugged a shoulder, maddeningly indifferent. "You believe it to be Thorburn?"

"I don't know who's behind it. Until I do, you must leave it to me. I thought you'd promised not to investigate on your own."

"I don't recall promising any such thing." She frowned and pressed her lips together. "I believe I have done well."

"Remarkably well." He cocked an eyebrow, slightly amused. "I don't have to worry about you, do I?"

Helen began to tidy the portfolio with her slim capable hands. "You have no need. I have a father, Lord Peyton, who will be home very soon." She raised her head. "Why do you care so much about us?"

Jason hesitated while he sought an effective answer. "I hold myself responsible for your safety and those in this house. It is your mother's wish. There are vulnerable people here, you especially, Lady Helen, because you've shown such an interest. There may be those who are growing impatient and nervous of discovery."

"I have only done what anyone in my position would do. In the absence of my mother and father." She pushed back the table, rattling the cups and saucers as she stood. "I am not a fool, Lord Peyton."

He rose and rested his hands lightly on her shoulders, feeling the tension in her body. Something had happened to this spirited girl who wanted so much more from life than the one she had chosen for herself. "I am aware of that," he murmured. Without thought, he traced her soft cheek with his knuckles. "I have never thought you foolish, Helen."

She hid her response to his touch beneath lowered lashes, but a telltale flush rushed up her throat, and she backed away until she came up against the desk. Recovering, she turned smartly back to the portfolio. "Could it be possible that someone has been reading this correspondence?"

"The library is open to anyone in the house, is it not?"

"Yes, but apart from the maids cleaning the rooms, no one could enter this room during the day without being seen. Therefore, they must come during the night. This new letter might draw them here." She fixed him with a stare. "Someone should spend the night and watch for them."

Jason raked his hands through his hair. "But it will not be you!"

Her gaze took in his disordered locks before answering. "There's no need to roar at me. I shall do it whatever you say."

"What!" He gave a slow grin at her sudden boldness. "If anyone spends the night here, it will be me."

She frowned. "Don't be so straight-laced. I am hardly a green girl. No one need know of it, and if they did, my reputation shan't suffer for none of the staff would repeat it outside this house."

"You have remarkable faith in your staff, Lady Helen," he said, his mouth an ironic twist. "I absolutely forbid it."

She glared. "You forbid it? I don't see how you will come to learn of it, Lord Peyton."

"Because we will keep watch together."

Helen stared at him. "But that's preposterous. Then I would be compromised, and so would you be."

"I am willing to take that chance."

She shook her head. "It's not necessary for you to be here. I have the perfect hiding place. No one will see me."

"Nevertheless, I expect you to admit me to the house after the butler has retired. I shall handle the night watchman. We must avoid the footman on night duty. You know how best to do that."

"I am not entirely sure I should allow you to—"

"Are you and your mother going out this evening?"

"No."

"Then Lady Kinsey will have retired by midnight?"

"Yes, but..."

"Then I'll be at the servants' entrance at midnight."

"No...I..."

"If you wish to obtain your mother's consent, please do so."

"But you know my mother will never agree to me spending the night in the library, let alone with you."

"I shall be there whatever you decide."

She frowned. "I..."

Behind them, the door opened. Jason turned as a bright head appeared. Lady Diana slipped into the room.

Jason bowed. "Lady Diana."

"Lord Peyton, how good to see you again." She hurried forward, her face wreathed in smiles.

Behind him, Helen shifted from her position at the desk. "You are too late for tea, Diana. Shall I ring for more?"

"Yes, please." Diana smiled brilliantly at him. "I was delighted to learn that you are attending my ball, Lord Peyton. I hope you will ask me to dance."

"I intend to, although I fear your beaux will claim them all." He smiled and turned to Helen. "Will you save me a waltz, Lady Helen?"

Helen's mouth, still tight with rigid disapproval at his authoritarian manner, softened. "I shall look forward to it."

He bowed. "I must leave you to enjoy your tea, ladies. My regards to Lady Kinsey."

Jason left the house with the certainty that Helen would be there to admit him. She had not agreed, but she would not leave him kicking his heels outside in the dark garden. Walking home, he considered his response to her question. Why did he care so much? He was only too aware of the feelings he had for her, which he was struggling to ignore, that grew stronger each day that passed. Heaven help him, he neither wanted the responsibility of another vulnerable female nor could he walk away from her. The guilt at his failure to prevent Phoebe from risking her life had never left him. Nor when he'd led his men into battle knowing he was taking many of them to their deaths.

Did he really want a peaceful life? After all it was he who wanted to continue with the investigation. He could hardly blame Parnell for that. He might well be wasting his time. But time was something he had plenty of lately, and for whatever reason, that no longer suited him. And while he was being entirely honest, he admitted that he was drawn to Kinsey House because of Lady Helen.

As he entered his front door, Lizzie, her eyes alight, ran to greet him. "Jas! I am engaged! Bianchi requests an interview with you."

He fought to hide his consternation. "My felicitations, Lizzie."

She eyed him speculatively. "You're not pleased."

"I have yet to form an opinion of Baron Bianchi."

"But you will not prevent the match?"

He sighed. Hard enough that he would lose her from his life, the man responsible was not his choice. He could not in all conscience prevent her taking a chance at happiness, however. "No, invite Bianchi to dinner on Friday."

"But that's days away."

"If he wants you, he will wait, Lizzie."

Jason retreated to his library, where he poured a liberal portion of whiskey into a tumbler, wrestling with these new feelings that almost overwhelmed him. Taking a deep sip, he leaned back in his chair and savored the blend of oak and peat on his tongue. After Phoebe's death and he'd left his angry father to join the army, he'd grappled for control of his emotions. And during the war, he succeeded. A man in charge of men could not afford to be emotional. It would get them killed. But it was as if from the moment of Parnell's accusation, that he was sleep walking through life, that he'd begun to thaw. He released a long breath, forced to admit he was greedy for passion and meaning in his life. With a faint

smile, he understood. Jason put down his glass. Well, that
was all going to change.

~ ~ ~

"Did I interrupt something between you and Peyton
when I came in?" Diana asked, arranging the flounced skirts
of her blue and white dimity gown as she joined Helen on
the library sofa.

"No, of course not." Helen settled her features into what
she hoped was a relaxed smile while trying to banish the
disturbing vision of spending a night alone with Peyton.
"Peyton has now turned his inquiries to an inn Bart used to
frequent. It's possible the tonic was tampered with there."

"Then Bart's death has nothing to do with us?"

"Maybe not."

"I must say I'm relieved." Frowning, Diana put down
her half-eaten muffin. "Still, the way Peyton looked at you
did not seem impersonal."

Helen's nervous fingers found the cameo brooch at her
neck. "We are merely trying to unravel this mystery in
Papa's absence. Mama wants it settled before the ball."

"He must have said something. You do not appear to be
your usual composed self." She tilted her head. "He wasn't
flirting with you?"

"Surely a man and woman can spend time together
without a romantic involvement?"

"But you must admit he's terribly attractive."

Helen began to stack the tea tray. She could not allow
herself to even dream of a future with Peyton. "You are such
a romantic. It's true that I do find him personable. But that's
all there is, so, please, do not embroider on it." Helen

yearned to be left alone to plan the evening. Could she manage somehow to remain dressed without Diana becoming suspicious? It seemed doubtful, and that would ruin everything.

"I don't know how you remain so remarkably unruffled, Helen. It is your nature, I suppose. Well, you may not want him, but I'm sure many women would. He has an air of authority, which fascinates, apart from being handsome. The combination of green eyes and dark locks is quite compelling. I could fall under his spell very easily."

"I'm sure he'd be pleased to hear you think so." Her chest grew tight. Jealousy was so unbecoming. She'd never considered herself capable of such a lowly emotion.

Diana smiled. "I might flirt with him if I could gain his attention."

"At the ball, you mean?"

Diana snorted. "When we dance, perhaps. But with you in the room, I tend to become invisible to him."

"What nonsense you talk." Helen stood, wishing to put a stop to the conversation, which made her nerves jangle. "What's that commotion in the hall? Has Mama arrived home?"

The door flung open, and Mama hurried in waving a letter. "This has just come from Walcott. Alexander has fallen from a tree."

They rushed over to her. "Is he badly hurt, Mama?" Helen asked.

"My dears!" Mama held out her arms and embraced them. "A broken limb they think. The doctor was with him when this letter was sent with your grandfather's carriage. The coachman is walking the horses. Eloise is packing a portmanteau. I must leave in a minute. Helen!" She held up a hand as Helen began to speak. "No, you cannot come. You are to remain here to chaperone your sister."

CHAPTER FIFTEEN

Helen listened to Diana's deep breathing. She had been asleep for over an hour, and it seemed safe to leave the bed. Earlier, while Helen was watched by her sister and their maid, Mary, she'd been forced to disrobe and don her nightgown. In the dark, Peyton wouldn't notice. She couldn't light a candle but was able to locate her dressing gown and slippers where she'd left them. Stealthily leaving the room, she hurriedly pulled them on, dislodging her nightcap in the process.

The candles were guttering in the wall sockets as she went to the stairway, her hair unraveling from the braid. Would he be waiting? At the bottom, she shivered. She rubbed her arms, unsure if it was the possibility of catching the thief or spending the night with Peyton that caused it. It would be better to send him away. But somehow, she doubted Peyton would obey her so easily.

The quiet kitchen lay in darkness with only the scuffle of cats on their nightly hunt. Something twined around her legs almost tripping her up and sending her heart into a gallop. "Quiet, Plato," she whispered at the cat's familiar greeting.

She slid the bolts back on the door, and a rush of chilly air blew her hair back from her face. Clutching her gown closer, aware that she wore little beneath it, she peered up at the inky blackness. Suddenly, a dark shape loomed into the doorway. Her heart in her mouth, she gave an involuntary squeak.

"*Shush.* You must have known it would be me." An iron-grip on her arm moved her aside as Peyton slipped inside.

"You might have been the thief." Indignant, she closed the door behind him, discarding any idea of deterring him. It would be a waste of her breath, which seemed to be in short supply.

"I've had a word with the watchman. He hasn't seen anyone, but the fellow seems to be too fond of rum by the smell of him."

"That's comforting." She was struggling to come to terms with receiving him in her nightclothes in the kitchen.

"It's too early for the thief. They would wait to be sure the whole household was asleep."

He sounded annoyingly pragmatic. "If he's a smart thief," she murmured, unwilling to let him have the last word as she led him up the stairs.

"He has been pretty clever up until now. And who's to say he isn't already in the house?"

She stopped so suddenly that he cannoned into her from behind.

When she gave a startled gasp, hands rested for a moment on her hips in her thin robe, causing her to stiffen. "You aren't going to panic are you, Lady Helen? I thought you were made of sterner stuff."

"And so I am, my lord," she said in a prickly tone, far too aware of his overly familiar gestures and big body close behind her.

"Are you sure the butler has gone to bed?"

"Yes. Fiske retired at eleven. Jeremy is in the front hall. He's good at dozing while remaining upright in his chair. I've caught him at it before."

"Then let's hope he does so tonight."

She opened the door to the library. With the deep burgundy velvet curtains pulled across the windows, the spacious room was black as pitch. Helen stumbled forward in what she guessed was the direction of the desk. "I shall have to light a candle until we are settled."

A hot flush rushed up her neck and spread across her face at the idea of settling somewhere in here for the night with this large ex-army man who was quite possibly a spy.

The cloak of darkness had its advantages. Men easily succumbed to their desires with a little encouragement. The worst of them needed none. And here she was in her nightclothes. How on earth did she get herself into this?

"No candles. I brought a rush light."

A tinder was struck, and a small glow lit up the room with a wisp of smoke. The Egyptian sarcophagus in the corner of the room took on a decidedly eerie appearance. Helen had considered hiding inside it but now shuddered at the prospect of entering that dark space where a mummy once rested.

"Where can we hide?" She distracted herself by gazing

around the dimly lit room. "Behind the sofa?"

"We can both fit in the coffin," Peyton observed in an exasperatingly calm tone.

"Don't be ridiculous!" She fought to keep her voice from rising to a hysterical pitch. "I am not getting in there with you."

"We'll leave the door open a crack."

"That isn't the problem."

In the faint light of the rush, his shadowed face loomed close to hers. "What is it then?"

"We would be…" She was unexpectedly lost for words.

"As close as birds in a roost? You have nothing to fear from me. I am not about to take advantage of the situation. I promise to keep my hands to myself."

"That isn't what I meant." Her cheeks were now so hot she might be sitting by the fire.

"What then?" He'd taken to roaming about the room and no longer seemed intent on her answer.

"It doesn't matter," she mumbled, realizing it was futile. They would never see eye to eye. She bent over the sofa to check the space behind it. "I can fit in here."

"These artifacts look quite atmospheric in this gloomy light," he murmured, right behind her. He peered into the dark space. "You could squeeze in there." His shoulder nudged hers. "But I cannot, and we need to be together so that we may confer."

"Confer?"

"Act together. As a force."

"This is not the army. We are not at war."

"We are in a way. We are fighting for justice, and this foe is a murderer," he said, sounding ruthless and quite unlike himself.

She shuddered again.

"Come and look inside." He swung the door of the sarcophagus open, and the smell of antiquity flowed out. "It's roomier than you think."

She swallowed. "I'm not..." she began. A scratching noise came from somewhere near the library door.

In the blink of an eye, Peyton had extinguished the rush light with his fingers and pulled her into the stone coffin, easing the door partly closed.

She took a deep breath of dusty stale air and something ancient, and indefinable, and clamped her mouth shut on a scream.

They waited, she hardly daring to breathe.

"Must have been mice behind the wainscoting," he finally whispered, making no attempt to leave. "But now that we're in here—"

Peyton appeared a good deal too pleased to be here. "It's too cramped." Aware of his spicy cologne and the touch of his leg against her bottom, Helen fought to remain calm. A hand alighted briefly on her side a whisker from her breast. She swallowed on a moan. The tension was excruciating.

Peyton cleared his throat. "Will you permit me to place my hands on your waist to support you? Otherwise, you might grow tired." His breathing sounded strained. He must find the air as stuffy as she did.

With her pulse galloping, Helen was tired already. This had been a ridiculous, fruitless exercise, and she had only herself to blame for it. "If you must."

She regretted it immediately. His hands seemed to burn into her flesh through her dressing gown. "Perhaps we might talk? If we keep our voices low, we can hear the door."

"Good idea," he said, his breath on her ear. "You have beautiful hair, Helen. It's very long and silky."

Helen launched into a rambling conversation. "I remember meeting your sister, Lady Greywood, years ago. She's very pretty and has a pleasant nature, as I recall." Not one of the spiteful debutantes Helen had encountered who had made her life hell. Elizabeth had Peyton's coloring. Dark hair and green eyes. "I was very sorry to hear of her loss."

"Thank you. Lizzie has only recently returned to society. I was very pleased to see it, but now, she's met someone."

He sounded worried. She wanted to turn and read his expression, which was foolish for they'd be pressed embarrassingly close together. "You don't like him?"

"I wish I could say I did." He sighed. "But Lizzie is keen to marry him and go to live in Italy."

She wanted to know more but could hardly ask. Was the fact that Elizabeth would leave England trouble him most?

"I can quite see why you'd be uneasy about it," she said. "You have a younger brother too, Viscount Brinkley."

"Charlie was recently sent down from Oxford for some prank. Fortunately, they've reinstated him. He's formed an unsuitable attachment to a Miss Groton, which has no future. I'm keen to see him finish his education and take the tour."

"Did you take the tour, or did the war intervene?"

"I took it." He chuckled.

"What amuses you?"

"The little I learned. But it is good for a young man to widen his horizons."

"You have no need to explain," she said hastily, guessing what he referred to.

His hands tightened at her waist. "I wasn't about to. I haven't forgotten I'm here with a lady." His voice dropped a notch, as if he found that difficult, which silenced her.

Almost an hour passed. Helen's legs began to grow tired, and she shuffled around in the small space allotted to her, careful not to tread on his big feet.

"We can't stand up all night," Peyton said, and for once, she had to agree with him. Although she doubted his solution to the problem would suit her.

"I'm perfectly all right," she said, fearing what he might suggest next.

There's room to sit if you'll perch on my lap."

"Are you always so frivolous?"

"Needs must. And perfectly aboveboard. To adopt a Naval term."

"You were never in the Navy."

"Here, I'll show you," he said with a soft chuckle. He sank down, pulling her with him onto his lap.

Before she could protest, he settled her across his knees, his hand touching parts of her that were just short of scandalous. She was sure he meant to do it. "There now, isn't that better? It's good that you're not wearing your corset. You can be comfortable. Lean back against me and close your eyes. If anything happens I'll wake you."

"Oh!" How dare he mention the absence of her

undergarments! Finding herself seated on muscular thighs and enveloped in strong masculine arms, Helen lost her ability to think of a suitable retort. Sleep? Was the man mad?

"I think we were mistaken. They're not coming." She struggled to rise without making matters worse. In the confined space, it proved impossible, and her elbow poked him in what she suspected with horror was a vital spot.

He groaned and tensed against her.

"Oh. I'm sorry, was that you…"

"It was." His voice sounded strained.

Beginning to feel quite giddy, she suffered a fit of the giggles. It must have been the stuffy interior, the masculine smell of him, or the fear that, if she remained here, she'd soon succumb to his charm.

"I'm glad you find it amusing. But please don't do that again." He moved carefully as if in discomfort, but there was laughter in his voice. "Keep still and be quiet."

She was in danger, but not from a foe, her own weakness. She liked being close to him far too much. How easy it would be to lean back against his strong chest and let nature take its course. She tensed with alarm at the direction her thoughts were taking. "I think I should leave," she whispered.

"An excellent idea. If you promise to go straight up to bed."

"Will you go home?"

"No. I'll stay awhile."

His hands vanished from where they'd rested on her diaphragm. "You know, you're a very comfy armful, Lady Helen, if I might be so bold."

"I think you've been quite bold enough." She knew she

sounded halfhearted. She could feel his chest shaking. He was laughing!

"I'm glad you find this amusing."

"As do you," he said with a chuckle.

"Perhaps a little," she agreed, a quiver in her voice betraying her. "This has all been very silly. A terrible idea of yours."

"I believe it was yours," Peyton said.

"I intended to spend the night behind the sofa, you will remember."

"As if I'd allow you to do a foolish thing like that."

"You would have no say in it, sir."

"No? You're in here with me, though, aren't you? Perhaps you prefer my company to the sofa's?"

She huffed. "You are not making sense. It must be the lack of fresh air." She began to wriggle forward. Once freed, she was sure she would think more clearly.

Peyton's hands slid farther around to enclose her diaphragm, halting her progress. "You know, Lady Helen, you and I would make a good team."

"Of detectives?" She paused, immediately caught by the suggestion.

"No, a woman could never be involved in dangerous work. A partnership certainly."

She stiffened. "I believe a woman would bring much to detective work. They have assets men lack."

"That's true, quite appealing endowments, and often a very shrewd mind, but I had a different partnership in mind."

"Really? I can't imagine..."

"Marriage," Peyton said firmly. "But I refuse to propose to you in this deuced coffin."

A fluttery, empty feeling settled in her stomach. She fought to sound brisk. "Don't be absurd. You really do need some fresh—"

A loud click made them freeze.

The library door opened, throwing faint light from the corridor wall sconces into the room. A vague shape appeared in her vision, creeping across the carpet to the desk. Peyton's hands tightened on her arms, his warning a mere breath on her hair. Caught up in the suspense, her pulse racing, she peered out through the crack.

After several fumbles, a candle burst into flame as another person shut the library door. Peyton's grip tightened. A dark-haired man she'd never seen before opened the portfolio, a candle raised to read Volta's letter. The other person came to join him. The first man cursed.

"He's ceased the experiments."

"What?" came a feminine voice. "Perhaps Kinsey will continue them with someone else. We should remain patient."

"It's grown too hot for us here," he snarled. "You should not have poisoned the maid. It is sure to arouse suspicion."

"She deserved it," Mrs. Chance said implacably.

Her words chilled Helen's blood. She sucked in a breath while Peyton squeezed her arm, although whether to silence her or reassure her, she wasn't sure.

"You enjoy killing too much, Charlotte," the man observed. "It makes you reckless."

"What are you saying, Pierre? It was you who poisoned

Bart's tonic. You can't blame me for that."

"It became urgent after you gave him that letter to deliver to me."

"How was I to know a footman could read French?"

Without warning, Peyton's hand on Helen's shoulder pressed her down. "Wait here until I call you." His quiet voice was like steel. From above her head came the sound of a pistol cocked. He pushed open the door of the sarcophagus and stepped out into the room.

"Move away from the desk and put your hands in the air," Peyton growled.

Both heads turned toward them. "*Mon Dieu*! Who the devil is this?" The man's menacing face looked almost ghoulish in the shadowy room.

"I didn't expect you to bother with us, Lord Peyton. Not with you and Lady Helen busily carrying on a treat."

Rage replaced her fear with a burning desire to confront the woman. Heedless of Jason's instruction, Helen flicked a lock of hair over her shoulder and abandoned the hiding place. "How careless of you to make that assumption, Mrs. Chance."

"Helen, raise Jeremy and send him for a constable," Peyton said. "And while we are waiting for the Watch, you two can enlighten me about your nasty little scheme."

Reassured by his imperturbable tone, Helen rushed to fling open the library door, closing it swiftly behind her. She was about to flee along the corridor when the flickering candlelight beneath the library door was suddenly extinguished.

A shot rang out.

~~~

Jason wasn't confident his shot found its mark in the dark. When the candle had gone out, a knife had whizzed past him, too close for comfort, and thwacked into the bookshelves behind him. He'd got off the shot before diving behind a chair. Crouching, he pulled out the knife he carried in his boot, cursing under his breath at not foreseeing the Frenchman's action. Helen must have heard the shot. For a moment, his fear that she would open the door and become a target, highlighted by the light from the corridor, brought his heart to his mouth. He couldn't risk calling out to her now; it might bring her running. Helpless, he waited. If anything happened to her... *If he lost her.* Why couldn't he have persuaded her to just stay in bed?

"Peyton?"

He slumped with relief. "Stay outside," he ordered, not confident she would obey him.

Loud sobs emanated from the end of the room, and he knew his shot had not gone wide. Bright candlelight flooded under the door and lightened the room to gray. He rose and moved cautiously toward the desk. Locating the fallen candelabra, he lit it. The man's prone body was spread-eagled on the floor. On her knees beside him, Mrs. Chance was patting his chest and making cooing noises.

Whirling around, Jason went to open the door. Helen's stricken white face greeted him, a branch of candles wavering and flickering in her hand.

"I thought it was you..." she said in a choked whisper, reaching out to touch his arm where his coat was torn.

"You're hurt." He looked down and saw blood. "I'll fetch a salve and some bandage. Jeremy has gone for the constable."

"I'm all right, just bring me a blanket."

Her eyes widened. "A blanket?"

"No questions, Helen. Just do it."

Jason returned to crouch beside the prone man. His ball had killed him instantly. Blank eyes stared sightlessly up at them.

Helen hurried in carrying the blanket.

When Jason threw it over the dead man, the housekeeper came to life. She launched herself at Jason, screeching like a banshee. He grabbed her wrists and held her until she wobbled and sank to the ground in a torrent of tears.

He hauled her over the sofa and sat her down. "Who is he?"

She sniffed. "The best man you're ever likely to meet."

"I doubt it. His name?"

"Pierre Valmay. My husband."

"You've been working together?"

She raised wild eyes to him. "Why should I tell you?"

"Better you tell me now then undergo the less polite treatment you'll receive at Bow Street."

"They'll hang me anyway," she said bitterly.

"Who hatched this plot?"

"Pierre did." For a moment, she looked triumphant and then slumped into despondency. "I overheard his lordship talking to Bart. He was describing his discovery and how it would be of immense value to England. When I told Pierre, he said he could sell the information to the French. And he would have, too, if you hadn't interfered. Pierre could do anything he set his mind on."

Jason flicked a glance at Helen. She was staring with fury at Mrs. Chance. "Why poison a harmless man like Bart?"

"We tried to persuade him to join us. With Lord Kinsey away for months, and with Bart's knowledge of the portfolio and his ability to access it at night, it was the perfect time to recruit him. But the fool refused. Said he was going to tell his lordship when he returned. He promised not to draw Lady Kinsey into it after we threatened to hurt her and the children. But we couldn't trust him."

"You're wicked!" Helen cried.

Mrs. Chance shrugged. "Bart must have realized his life was in danger, for I heard him asking Jeremy to deliver a letter to Whitehall. Then Pierre began following Bart, waiting for a chance to kill him without rousing suspicion. An opportunity to poison his tonic arose at the Lamb and Flag. Pierre paid a man to provoke Bart into a fight." She stared up at them, and her expression became one of great cunning. "When Bart grew too ill to meet you and knew he wouldn't live, he wrote a letter for Lord Kinsey. Hid it in his Bible. As if I wouldn't find it!"

"We discovered the scorched remains of his letter in the fireplace," Jason said. "You left enough to give us a vital clue."

For a moment, her eyes burned with hatred, and then she dropped her gaze to her hands.

"You might have killed Alice, who did nothing to hurt you." Helen's voice was low and hard with anger.

"It was a warning," Charlotte Chance said. "Just to get her out of the way."

"I don't believe you!" Helen came closer, her hands coiled into fists, her breast rising and falling with her agitated breath. "You *wanted* to hurt Alice because she had defied you."

Watching with amazement and pride, Jason stepped closer in case he needed to restrain Helen should she try to hit the woman. She stared down at Mrs. Chance with intense loathing. "You deserve everything that is coming to you."

The door opened to admit the constable.

"Most of the household will be awake. I'd best go and speak to them, but first I want to tend your wound." Helen turned and left the room.

Several hours past dawn, Helen had managed to dress and wake Diana. The house was still in an uproar after the coroner left and the body was removed. An officer from Bow Street took Charlotte Chance away in the wagon.

At the front door, with Helen's expertly applied bandage covering a long but shallow knife wound, Jason placed his good arm around her. "You were magnificent. Now you should go to bed. You must be exhausted."

She turned her vivid gaze up to him, her inviting lips curling in a smile. "I've never felt so alive. We have avenged Bart."

"You are right, sweetheart."

"About what you said in the sarcophagus," she began. "You must—"

"I meant every word." He drew her close and planted a

kiss on her mouth.

A lanky gentleman with sunburned skin paused at the gate. "This is what occurs when my back is turned?" he cried, stalking down the path.

"Papa!" Helen ran and threw her arms around him.

Brilliant blue eyes flicked from Jason's sleeve to his face. "Lord Peyton? What are you about kissing my daughter in full view of the street?"

"We need to talk, sir," Peyton began.

"Papa, Lord Peyton has been wonderful. He —" Helen rushed to explain.

Kinsey held up a hand. "The coach lost a wheel on the outskirts of London. I have endured a bumpy ride in a horrible reeking hackney for some hours. I require coffee and food. Where is your mother? Surely it's too early for her to embark on one of her charity affairs?"

"No, Mama is at Walcott. Alexander has broken his leg."

"Dear heaven, the poor boy! Can't I leave you all alone for a few weeks?"

"I'm afraid there's more to tell, Lord Kinsey," Jason said.

"Please join us for breakfast, Lord Peyton." He swept his daughter inside.

In the breakfast room, Lord Kinsey, having disposed of a large breakfast of kidneys, bacon, and eggs, leaned back in his chair, his fingers linked over his stomach. "That's an extraordinary story." He shook his head. "Poor Bartholomew. I liked him very much. Intelligent and brave. He certainly didn't deserve such a fate."

"No, he did not." Jason planned to tell Kinsey about his experience of Bart during the war. But that could wait.

"But, Papa, Volta has written," Helen said. "He's

decided not to continue working with you."

"Oh well. As to that. I've already come to the same conclusion, having discovered something with greater promise. I can't wait to begin my research and shall look for a likely inventor to join me in my quest."

"What quest, Papa?" Diana asked.

Her father waved a hand. "Flight my dear! I've discovered the Ancient Egyptians had some excellent notions about man being able to fly. I have brought copious notes and diagrams home with me."

"Men will fly one day, Papa? How utterly fascinating," Helen said. "I would really like to assist you with this new discovery, if I may?"

"I must say that surprises me, Helen." He smiled. "I never suspected for a moment that my work would interest you."

"But it does. I should like to accompany you on your next voyage."

"Mm?" He patted her hand. "Would you indeed? I believe you have regained some of your spirit, my girl." He turned to Jason. "Now, sir. You have explained your reasons for spending the night in my library more than adequately. I am extremely grateful for the outcome, if not the method employed." He laughed. "But I imagine you found it difficult to persuade Helen to remain out of it! However, you have yet to explain your overly familiar attitude toward her, which goes well beyond the bounds of propriety."

"I fully intend to, sir. But first, I would like to speak to Lady Helen alone," Jason said. "If you'll permit me."

Looking troubled, Helen shook her head. "You have no need, Lord Peyton. There is nothing to be said."

"I have every need." Jason smiled at her. He wished there had been more time to do the thing properly. The ball would have been the perfect place to declare himself, having first danced her out onto the terrace, but it couldn't be helped. Kinsey was not going to wait for that, and Jason couldn't either. He threw caution to the winds, even while sensing it was too soon. But patience wasn't one of his attributes. He needed to know *now* if Helen would become his wife.

Lord Kinsey's warm smile encompassed them both. "It appears you have spent a great deal of time alone in each other's company. I don't see why a half-hour more will hurt. Please repair to the morning room. I require my library." He stood and rubbed his hands. "Thorburn will be here soon, and there is much to be done."

As they all trouped out of the breakfast room, Kinsey turned to Diana. "Is everything in readiness for your ball, my dear?"

Diana's eyes filled with tears. "I'm not sure, Papa. Our housekeeper has gone to prison, and Mama isn't here."

"I will take over the housekeeper's duties," Helen said. "I have no need to appear at the ball."

"You will attend it though, daughter," Lord Kinsey said, brooking no argument.

He put his arm around Diana's shoulders. "Your mother will return in time, and your ball shall be the most celebrated of the Season. I only hope Alexander recovers well. A broken leg is not something to sneeze at."

As the morning room door closed behind them, Helen

turned to Jason. "I did warn that we might be compromised. But fortunately, my father is a reasonable man. I believe he likes you. So please, do not feel you have anything to reproach yourself for."

"I'm aware of that." Stepping close, he raised her chin with a finger when she refused to meet his gaze. "I did not wish it to be under these circumstances. I would have chosen a more romantic course, but I care for you, Helen. Will you marry me?" Her eyes were dark, troubled. He'd hoped to find some sign of acceptance and at least affection, but her anguish turned his blood to ice. This was all too soon.

She attempted to move away. "I cannot marry you, Peyton."

He caught her, making her stay. "Are you denying there's more than fondness between us?"

"I consider you to be a friend. I am very grateful for everything you've done for us."

"You're grateful? This is not merely a friendship. And I won't accept your gratitude!"

He cradled her face in his hands. Swooping down, he took her mouth. This was not to be a polite kiss. He cupped the back of her head, drawing her closer. Moving his mouth over hers, he learned the shape of her soft lips, delighting in her response. His blood heated and rampaged through his veins as he ran his tongue along the seam of her lips. When she made a small sound and opened to him, he slipped inside, the sweet taste of her mouth sending his blood swirling. Helen sagged against him. When she made a sound close to a sob, her arms crept up around his neck and her fingers twined in his hair.

He murmured encouragement and kissed her throat, beneath her ear, and, with a moan, returned to ravage her mouth. When he finally drew away, he smiled into her wistful eyes. "Can you still say ours is a friendship?"

Her cheeks were rosy, and her breath came fast, but she moved away from him, her fingers working to tidy her disordered locks. "You are a very attractive man, Peyton. I admit to enjoying your kisses. But I shan't marry you."

He fought to cool down and released a long sigh. "Is there someone else?"

"No. I shall never marry. I plan to travel with my father. I am confident he will permit me to accompany him now." She sounded strained.

He watched, frustrated that she held herself aloof from him. "He might. But I gained the impression he'd rather you married."

"Papa will grow used to the idea in time. And if he doesn't, I shall remain at Cherrywood. I would rather spend the spring there than anywhere."

He didn't understand her. Didn't believe her. "You are sure this is what you want?"

Turned away from him, her voice was muffled. "Yes, it is."

"As you wish." He bowed. "If you'll excuse me, there are matters at home I must attend to."

He left her and went to the library.

Learning of Helen's refusal, Lord Kinsey shook his head with bemusement. "I am surprised and disappointed. But her mother will handle this. We men are somewhat lacking in these matters, are we not? I hope to see you, Lady Greywood, and your brother, Charles, at the ball."

Jason made his way to the front door. He doubted Helen would get her wish to accompany her father on his travels. Kinsey was determined she marry. Having decided Jason was the man he wanted for her, he made it plain that he had not yet given up hope.

There was something here he didn't understand. Recalling her decided preference for his kisses, Jason wasn't going to give up hope either.

"Your hat, Lord Peyton. The gardener found it in the shrubbery," Fiske said politely, handing it to him at the door. "If I may speak for the staff, we are all very grateful to you, sir."

"Thank you, Fiske." Peyton jammed the hat on his head and strode out the door.

CHAPTER SIXTEEN

Diana opened the morning room door and peeked in, her face alive with curiosity. "Well? Did you accept him?"

Helen was sitting very still on the sofa, gazing into space. "No."

Her sister plopped down beside her. "You didn't? You refused that magnificent man? After he saved us all? After he declared his love for you?"

Helen stared down at her hands. "He didn't say he loved me."

"Did you give him a chance to?"

"There was no point. I am not going to marry him."

"Why ever not?" Diana shook her head. "I don't understand you at all. You never show any emotion. Don't you want to be in love? To be loved? Love is the most glorious sentiment on the earth!"

Afraid to answer, Helen sagged in her chair and fiddled with the braid on her sleeve.

"Do you really want to become one of those spinsters with a dozen cats?" Diana persisted. "And live at Cherrywood caring for Harry until he marries? And once he marries, knit items for your nieces and nephews? I suppose you could then take care of Toby when he is a young bachelor. Is that a life worth living?"

"Stop!" Helen leaped up, tears coursing down her cheeks. She sucked in a shaky breath. "I would very much like to be married. Married to Peyton, if you must insist on having me admit it!" She covered her eyes with her hands, her shoulders shaking with sobs.

Diana hurried to hug her. She pulled the damp hair from Helen's face. "Then why won't you accept him?"

Helen drew away with a hiccup. "Because he believes me to be untouched."

Diana gaped at her. "You're not a virgin? When on earth did that happen? Who was it?"

Her eyes awash with tears, Diana's image blurred. Helen gulped to relieve the ache at the back of her throat. "Remember my first Season when I came home ill with that head injury?"

"It was then? No one would tell me anything."

"Of course not. You were thirteen years old. It was hardly fitting."

"I am not thirteen now."

"It was at my first ball. I foolishly went into the garden with a man, and he, and he..." She bit her lip.

Diana took her hand and led her back to the sofa. "He hurt you? Who was it?"

"Lord Lawley. I struggled with him and hit my head. I don't remember much about it."

"It's a wonder Papa didn't have him thrown in

Newgate."

Helen shook her head. "Papa doesn't know the extent of it. Only that the man made ill-mannered advances to me and I panicked." She covered her face with her hands. "He now thinks me timid and doesn't respect me, although I know he loves me."

"Then why didn't Mama tell him?"

"She was afraid if he knew he would call Lawley out. He is younger and known to be a good shot. Papa would have been killed. Then Lawley left the country, and it was too late."

"But Mama wants you to marry. She often says so."

"She wants me to put the past behind me. I cannot do that, Diana. I would have to tell my prospective husband the truth. I'm too ashamed."

Diana muttered one of their brother's favorite curses. "I don't see why you should feel ashamed. It was entirely that rake's doing." She raised an eyebrow. "You know, I don't think Peyton would care, although I'm pretty sure he would go after Lawley."

"He would." Helen curled her fingers into her palms. "That's what I'm afraid of."

"Peyton can handle himself. Certainly, he is better able to than some dissolute rake."

"I can't be sure of that. He might get hurt, or worse. The whole thing would be utterly horrifying."

She gripped Helen's shoulder. "But, dearest, only think. This dreadful attack has blighted your life. I thought you had no passion in you. That has changed since Peyton came here. And I, for one, approve!"

"Nevertheless," Helen said, drawing in a shuddering

breath. She didn't have the energy and thought it unwise to tell the whole of it. "I won't subject Peyton to that. I have made up my mind."

~~~

In no mood to deal with his siblings, Jason eyed Charlie with a frown. "Why are you seated behind my desk, drinking my best brandy?"

With an apologetic shrug, Charlie removed his feet from the leather desktop. He vacated Jason's chair and dropped onto the sofa, brandy glass in hand. "I have had some unwelcome news," he said with a lowering glance as Jason took the seat and sorted through his mail.

"Oh?" Jason found it hard to raise a level of interest.

Putting down his empty glass, Charlie folded his arms and leaned back to study him. "You look in even worse shape than me."

"Do I? I can't look too good then. I hope you'll abandon that affecting Brutus and get your hair cut before you return to university."

"Amelia Groton has just married some aging nabob," Charlie said, emphasizing every syllable.

Jason put down the pearl-handled letter opener. Seeing Charlie's bloodshot eyes, he suffered a moment's anguish for his young brother, knowing how much rejection hurt at that age, and even at thirty-two, it still cut like a knife. "I'm sorry, Charlie. I really am."

"I'll survive, Jas." He unfolded his long legs. "Shall I pour you a brandy?"

"If you would." Jason sliced open a letter from Mr. Gillies. It appeared that the expert, John Smith, considered the Albrecht Dürer work to be a forgery. He frowned and tapped the knife on his blotter. This opened a Pandora's box, and he would have to act quickly to deal with it before he met with Bianchi. He put the letter to one side and opened another. It was from his friend, Robert Vale, in Italy. He quickly perused it. "Good God!"

Charlie handed him the tumbler of brandy. "What is it?"

"Is Lizzie at home?"

"Yes. She's organizing her wardrobe for Italy. You know, I still haven't taken to her fiancé. Do you like him?"

"Go and fetch her, will you? You'll have to wait until I've spoken to her, Charlie. Alone."

Charlie accepted this request with newly acquired patience and departed on the errand.

Jason read the letter again. It appeared that all three Peytons were to suffer some measure of heartbreak. Vale's letter from Florence was unequivocal. *I'm a trifle confused by your letter, Jason. Bianchi is here in Florence. Spoke to him yesterday as a matter of fact. As to the drawing by Albrecht Dürer, I've never seen one in his collection. And I must say I know every one of his pieces almost by heart.*

Lizzie came in some minutes later. She glanced at his face and then at the letter he held. "It's unwelcome news, isn't it? I feared it might be."

After reading the letter, she shook her head in confusion. "Does this mean that the Bianchi we know is not the real one?"

"There can be no other explanation." His hands formed into fists as a tear ran down Lizzie's cheek.

"But why would he want to marry me under false pretenses?"

Jason had employed the few minutes while he was alone to consider that. The answer was too dreadful to voice. "He's a forger, Lizzie. And he doesn't work alone. I suspect this Barrett is in league with him. He's most likely the artist behind the works."

"But still, it doesn't explain..." Her face grew pale, and she bit her lip. "Once we married and he took me away, he could take control of my fortune, couldn't he?"

"Yes, he could," he said gently. And heaven only knew what the nasty piece of work would do to Lizzie when he had complete control over her. Jason tamped down his wrath and moved to the sofa to comfort her.

She took his proffered handkerchief and blew her nose. "How dreadful," she murmured. "And to think I believed him. How gullible am I?"

"I thought he might be a fraudster, but never for one moment suspected this. I will deal with him. You will never see the man again."

"You're probably right that I shouldn't see him. But how much I would like to. If only to spit in his eye," Lizzie said, with a sharp intake of breath.

"That's the Lizzie I know," he said with a smile. He was pleased to see she still had spirit.

Charlie came into the room. "Is everything all right?"

"Sit down, Charlie," Jason said. "Your instincts have been proven right about Bianchi."

After dinner, when Charlie had taken himself off, Jason sat with Lizzie in the library.

"I'd forgotten to ask you about Lady Diana Kinsey," Lizzie said. "Since we're invited to her debutante ball on Saturday evening, I hope that, at last, you might be considering what you reluctant gentleman term the parson's mousetrap."

He rubbed a hand through his hair. "No. Not Lady Diana. Lady Helen. But she has refused me,"

With a concerned huff, Lizzie frowned. "She refused you? For what reason? I'm surprised any woman in her right mind would do that."

"Well, thank you, Lizzie," he said with a ghost of a smile. "But alas it is true. Do you know Lady Helen?"

"I have met her. She came out a year or so after me. She was one of the more interesting debutantes, amusing. I remember her first Season. Very sad business."

"How so?"

"You don't know?"

"Evidently I don't. Are you going to enlighten me?"

"Apparently, that rakehell, Albert, Lord Lawley ravaged her in the Chillinghams' garden. She hit her head and was taken home to the country concussed. I last saw Lady Helen at Lady Newley's ball, just before Greywood died. She seemed very much changed, quite subdued, and, to my knowledge, didn't dance."

"Lawley, you say? Jason growled.

"Yes. His father was furious. Lawley left England shortly afterward."

"How wise of him." He thought for a minute. "Godwin at Horse Guards was a cohort of his. They were known to hunt in a pack, picking on vulnerable women. Nasty pieces of work the lot of them. I wonder…"

She eyed him carefully. 'What will you do about Bianchi? You are not to call him out, Jason. I couldn't bear it."

He sighed with frustration, wanting to take the man apart piece by piece. "Very well. I don't have the authority to arrest him. I'll notify the Bow Street magistrate. He'll invite Bianchi, or whatever his real name is, and his accomplice, in for questioning. I'll alert Mr. Gillies, whom I expect will want to learn of this and give evidence if required. Mr. Smith, the foremost expert in art forgery, might be willing to inspect the rest of the works, although I suspect many would have been sold."

When Lizzie, who seemed more relieved than heartbroken, left the room, Jason, at last, allowed his thoughts to dwell on Helen. Learning what had happened to her all those years ago explained so much. He intended to broach the subject with her. He would have the truth. Was it because of her past that she wouldn't have him? He could deal with that, for although he was in a murderous rage at what had happened to her and would happily run the man through, it didn't matter a damn to him if he wasn't the first. But if she did not love him, he would have to accept it. Strange, how his once-wished-for, quiet life now seemed so dashed unpalpable.

CHAPTER SEVENTEEN

On Friday, Mama arrived home with Toby. "Kinsey!" She rushed into Papa's arms in the entry where Helen and Diana stood waiting to greet her.

Papa enveloped her in a hug. "How is Alexander?"

"Healing well. He prefers to remain with his grandfather, and I thought it wise not to make him endure a journey in the coach." She leaned back to scrutinize him. "Have you been wearing your hat? You're as brown as a nut."

He laughed and swung her around in his arms. "And you are even more beautiful than I remember."

Diana grinned at Helen, as their mother, ignoring Fiske, who was examining his shoes, ran her hand through their father's copper locks, sprinkled with gray. "You have not forgotten how to charm a lady, I'm pleased to see." She turned to Helen. "When the footman delivered your note, I was utterly horrified. I do hope you weren't in danger?"

Helen kissed her mother's cheek. "Not for a minute." Helen continued to try, unsuccessfully, to banish all thoughts of Peyton. It was unlikely after the ball they would meet again.

"I am eternally grateful to Lord Peyton for dealing with this. *Mrs. Chance!* Just imagine. When she came to us a year ago after Mrs. Archer retired and went to live with her sister, she presented perfect references. Can we no longer trust anyone?" She studied Helen's face then gave a quick nod. "We will talk later."

"The staff expects me at eleven. I must go over the final details before the ball," Helen said, relieved to have a reprieve before she came under her mother's sagacious scrutiny. One word about Peyton and she feared she would dissolve into a puddle like one of Cook's sculptured ices.

Mama smiled. "Thank you, Helen dear. You are a blessing. I am too exhausted and bewildered to be of much use until I have had a nap to refresh me."

Papa eyed her speculatively for a minute before addressing Toby. "My boy, it is good to see you. I trust you are pleased to be home?"

"I am, Papa. Catching tadpoles for Zander and playing cribbage with Grandfather had begun to pall."

Her father laughed and ushered them into the morning room. Papa sipped a glass of claret Fiske handed him and, prompted by Toby, related the fascinating highlights of his journey. Wishing she could remain to hear every detail, Helen reluctantly excused herself.

Diana followed Helen out and slipped an arm around her waist as they walked toward the servants' stairs. "Thank you for taking over from Mrs. Chance. Even though Papa has requested the employment agency send someone, it is far too late."

Helen smiled. "'Tis my pleasure."

"You have a natural talent for it, I must say. It would bore me to distraction." Diana paused, a hand on the newel post. "You'll make an excellent wife and mother, running your own household."

Pain clawed at Helen's heart. "Please don't, Diana. I beg you."

"For a sensible person, you are being remarkably dull-witted," Diana said fiercely. "I hope that Peyton will shake some sense into you!"

Helen watched her sister stalk away. Diana was young and had little understanding of how damning and cruel society could be. She prayed Diana would never experience it as she continued down the stairs. Might it be possible that Peyton would ask her again? She both feared and welcomed it. She could not deny that when he'd kissed her she'd responded with unrestrained passion, her normally practical mind deserting her. She hadn't wanted his kisses to end, and it had taken all her strength to push him away. If he'd remained a minute longer, she might have weakened and thrown herself into his arms.

A sleepless night brought no solution, leaving her feeling as if she was floating, rudderless in a stormy sea. But to tell him of her past and see the respect he had for her fade from his green eyes would be the end of her.

In the servants' hall, everyone waited, having responded to her summons. She looked around at the group of expectant faces. "Good morning." She managed to sound proficient.

An hour later, confident that every last detail had been

seen to, Helen reluctantly made her way upstairs. She met her father in the corridor leaving her mother's boudoir. He winked. "Listen to your mother's advice, daughter. She is never wrong."

"Yes, Papa."

Inside the bedroom, her mother sat alone at the dressing table in her wrap, coiling her hair into a chignon. Her face reflected in the glass bore a healthy flush.

"How is Alexander, Mama? And Grandfather? Did you leave them in good health?"

"Grandfather is well. Alexander's leg was not broken. It's merely a bad sprain. He is healing well, although it will take a month or so before he has completely recovered. We'll talk more about that later." She turned on the stool. "Your father tells me you have refused Lord Peyton."

"Yes." Helen groaned inwardly and sank onto the sofa.

Mama rose to join her. "But why, my dear? It's an excellent match. And not because he's an earl; he cares for you."

"He believes I am something I'm not."

"Nonsense. He knows exactly who you are. A dear sweet, caring person. I believe he needs a bit of mothering himself."

"Peyton?" Helen was shocked. She never thought of him that way. He was so commanding, so confident. "He's a hardened soldier." The suggestion that he might need her was enticing, and she fought not to let it sway her decision.

"Peyton's mother died giving birth to his brother. He has been away at war, and now that his father is gone, he is head of the family with all the responsibilities that entails. Who cares for Peyton? He may not be aware that he needs it. Men are inclined to be blind to such things. They feel they must be strong all the time. And find solutions for everything." She smiled. "But even your intrepid father needs my support and comfort. While I need his strength." Mama's eyes grew misty. "And his love."

Helen leaned close and breathed in her mother's familiar flowery scent, which was usually reassuring, although not today. "But it wouldn't be fair to him. He would feel that because he's asked for my hand, and addressed Papa, he is committed to marrying me."

"I think you underestimate Peyton."

"I...I don't believe I do."

"He has a good deal of character. I like him very much, and so does your father."

"Yes. I thought he did."

"I know you feel you're doing the honorable thing, my dear. But love, and I am sure Peyton does love you, can overcome most obstacles. Will you promise me that you'll at least reconsider his offer?" Mama placed an arm around her. "I've been observing the two of you and believed..." She sighed. "I had such hopes for you, dear child."

What good would it do, when the answer must always be the same? "I promise, Mama." Helen rested her head on her mother's shoulder and sadly resisted saying anything more.

~~~

Russell appeared at the breakfast room door. "Mr. Dalby from Bow Street is here to see you, my lord."

Jason looked up from the newspaper he was reading, his kippers half eaten. "Send him in, Russell." He motioned to the footman for more coffee and pushed his plate away, his appetite deserting him.

The runner hurried into the room still in his greatcoat, hat in hand. "Sorry to bother you so early, Lord Peyton, but the magistrate wanted to alert you to the fact that the man claiming to be Baron Bianchi has slipped the net."

Jason pushed back his chair. "How did he manage to do that? He was here in London yesterday." And tonight, Bianchi expected to be granted Lizzie's hand. "What caused him to run?"

"We don't know, milord. We went to his digs this morning and discovered he'd packed up and left some hours before."

"Could he have known you were after him?"

"One of our men followed him last night, but he gave him the slip. Must have got wind of it."

Jason tightened his jaw. "Your man must have stood out like a sore thumb."

"It appears that Bianchi, so called, and another gentleman left in a carriage several hours ago, milord. Traveling north to Liverpool."

"Where are they off to, Ireland or New York?" Jason mused. "They're after fresh pickings, eh, Dalby." Jason did not have the authority to arrest Bianchi. He'd need the runner to accompany him. "Care to pursue them?"

Dalby pulled back his greatcoat and indicated the gun that runners always carried with them. "Left my horse in your stables. I'm keen, milord."

Jason turned to the footman. "Henry, send word to the groom. I want Icarus saddled. Dalby, there's coffee in the pot. Help yourself. We shall leave in a few minutes."

He ran up to Lizzie's rooms.

"Lady Greywood has just left for Madam Bernard's salon in Oxford Street," Sally said. "She needs an alteration to her ball gown."

Jason cursed under his breath. "Why didn't you accompany her?"

"Milady wished me to finish some mending." She flushed and eyed a corset on the table beside her workbasket.

Jason went to bang on Charlie's door then remembered his brother had stayed with a friend the previous evening after attending a bachelor dinner.

He needed first to alert Lizzie. It seemed likely that Bianchi intended to quit England. But he didn't trust the Italian not to try some sneaky ploy. Hopefully, he and Dalby, riding hard, could overtake their carriage in a matter of hours. It depended on whether Bianchi thought he'd got away with it and was traveling at a leisurely pace or making flat-out for Liverpool. If it was the latter, Jason might not return to London until the early hours of the morning. As he left with Dalby, Jason preferred the former, considering the forger's over developed sense of his own capabilities.

His only chance to change Helen's mind was the ball tonight. If he failed to appear, he feared he might not get another.

In Oxford Street, Jason left Dalby with the horses and strode into Madam Bernard's salon, causing a lady to shriek and disappear behind a curtain.

Madam Bernard erupted from a dressing room, moving with surprising speed for one so well endowed. "Milord?"

"Madam. I believe my sister, Lady Greywood, is here?"

"Yes. Milord." The modiste turned and addressed the stunned servant with her. "Annie, fetch Lady Greywood. "Would you care to take a seat in the salon, Lord Peyton? A glass of wine, perhaps?"

Relieved to find Lizzie safe, Jason tamped down his impatience, keen to continue his pursuit. "No, thank you."

Madam Bernard twisted the tape measure around her neck with her fingers. "Then if you'll excuse me, I'll see if I can assist Lady Greywood."

"Thank you."

As Jason stalked the now empty salon, Lizzie hurried from the dressing room in her wrap. "Jason! What has happened?"

He quickly explained and told her to go home as soon as she could and stay there. "I shall endeavor to return in time to escort you to the ball."

She placed a hand on Jason's arm, her eyes dark. "Oh, Jason. You must want to see Lady Helen tonight. This is all my fault. You will take care, won't you?"

"None of this is your fault, Lizzie. There's nothing to fear. I have an able-bodied runner with me."

He joined Dalby, and they rode through the London streets. "It rained heavily during the night," Jason said. "The muddy roads might slow the carriage up."

Dalby nodded. "We'll get 'em, yer lordship."

"I want to bring them back alive, Dalby," Jason called before taking advantage of the clear stretch ahead. He squeezed his horse's flanks, urging Icarus into a gallop.

"Right you are," Dalby replied as he rode alongside him. "Providing they come peaceable like."

CHAPTER EIGHTEEN

"By God, you have sired a pair of beauties, Kinsey!"
Lord Nicholas smiled at Helen and Diana as he stood at the
ballroom door with their parents to receive the first of the
guests. Helen curtseyed, and Diana, giggling, followed suit.
One could always count on Uncle Nicholas for his support.
His kind words were appreciated, but it was Diana's beauty
that would eclipse every young woman here tonight. Diana
hadn't wished to wear white, but the silk sheath clung to her
tall elegant figure and was the perfect foil for her fresh
beauty, setting off her copper ringlets caught up with satin
ribbon and silk rosebuds.

As Fiske announced the guests, Helen searched for
Peyton. By ten o'clock, the last guests had arrived, and the
doors were closed. The ballroom was packed with people,
the crystal chandelier showering a myriad of dancing lights
upon the convivial crowd. As she walked through the room,
she caught snatches of conversation about George IV's
coronation which was to be held in July, and how Queen

Caroline was prevented from attending.

Pleased not to be the subject of gossipers, Helen took note that the hired waiters were doing as instructed, threading their way through the guests with trays bearing glasses of brandy and claret punch. The Master of Ceremonies announced a quadrille, and the orchestra sprang to life on the dais.

A large group of gentlemen immediately converged on Diana. She gracefully accepted a young marquess' son who had been introduced to her moments before. Helen caught her mother's eye and smiled. She turned to where Fiske stood alone at the door. Peyton had not come. It didn't surprise her; she'd been very convincing in her refusal of his proposal. If only she'd convinced herself! Was it possible for a heart to actually ache?

A distant cousin of her mother's, newly widowed, approached Helen, and forcing a smile, she took his arm. Tonight was Diana's, and she must never allow her misery to become obvious.

An hour later, Helen entered the supper room to ensure that everything was in readiness for the guests. Tempting aromas wafted through the room. The white-linen-covered tables were laden with delectable hot and cold dishes; a tureen of white soup, collared beef, artichoke hearts, silver salvers of lobster, pyramids of crayfish, and sandwiches. Luscious trifles and sweet meats sat amid fine crystal and china, sparkling silverware, and silver urns of decorative fruits and flowers. Gilt chairs lined the walls for the guests, and servants stood ready to serve them claret, champagne, sherry, hock, or port.

Helen went in search of her parents, only to find Peyton

talking to them, his dark good looks set off to perfection by his midnight black evening clothes and sparkling white cravat. His sister, the dark-haired Lady Greywood, stood beside him dressed in deep violet, with a handsome young gentleman of similar coloring who must be Charlie.

Helen stood for a moment unsure whether to join them. Aware she blushed, she tried to tamp down her delight at finding him here. Peyton's eyes lifted to hers. He sent her a special smile as if they shared a secret. She returned his smile with a shy one of her own but had no idea what she would say to him; she was just so very glad to see him. She began to make her way through the groups of chatting people.

Peyton bowed over her hand. "Lady Helen. I believe you know my sister?"

"I do. Lady Greywood, how delightful to see you again."

"And you, Lady Helen."

"I should like to introduce you to my brother, Viscount Brinkley," Peyton said.

Charles bowed before her. His charming smile would interest the ladies.

"I must apologize. We are unforgivably late." Lizzie fiddled with her fan, her eyes shadowed. "My brother has only just returned to London."

"You were called away, my lord?" Helen asked.

"Yes. Unexpectedly." He held out his arm. "The musicians are about to play, Lady Helen. I believe you promised me a waltz?"

They joined the swirling dancers. Helen slipped into his arms, feeling as if she belonged there.

"Lizzie's suitor turned out to be a rogue," Peyton explained. "An imposter who forged and sold art." He reversed her expertly in a swift turn.

Helen gained her breath, only to lose it again when she met his intense green eyes. "That is a dreadful shame. Lady Greywood did appear downhearted." What had occurred earlier in the evening? Had Peyton come into danger? Would he tell her if he had? "You went to apprehend him?"

"It was necessary to bring the fellow to justice. Lizzie is disappointed naturally but also greatly relieved to have discovered the truth in time. A Bow Street runner and I caught up with them on their way to Liverpool." He smiled down at her "But that's a story for another time." His eyes softened. "You look lovely tonight. You should wear that color often. In fact, I rather fancy picking a posy of lilacs for you in the woods at Peyton Grove."

"That is a nice thought." She was blushing again, but she didn't care. Just being in his arms had turned the night into something magical.

"It can become a reality if you would say yes."

She couldn't deal with this now and struggled to find a change of topic. "Charles seems rather like you."

He widened his eyes. "You think so?"

"He has that devil-may-care air."

Peyton grinned. "I'm not sure that's a compliment."

She laughed and glanced over to where Charles flirted with a shy young debutante. "He seems to have recovered well from the disappointment over Miss Groton."

"The young bounce back." He tightened his clasp on her

hand. "We older gentlemen do not."

Despite his flippant words, he looked troubled, making her want to reach up to touch his cheek. Knowing she was the cause of it, she almost couldn't bear it. "Peyton, I—"

"Shall we talk when there is no one to overhear us?" he asked, his deep, sensual voice sending tingles through her.

For a moment, she'd almost forgotten where they were. That they were surrounded by an interested audience who had not seen her dance for several years.

When the music died away, Peyton led her from the dance floor. "Will you come with me to the terrace?"

That was entirely too risky. She didn't trust herself. "My parents will notice."

"Does it matter? However, I have my doubts. My brother has just made a beeline for your sister."

"Oh?" Helen laughed. "He will have to stand in line."

"We Peytons are patient souls."

"Are you? I don't remember noticing that quality in you, sir."

"Not always. Not when there is something we very much want." He tucked her hand in the crook of his arm. "Will you come?"

"I need to visit the supper room to make sure everything is going smoothly."

"There's no need." He put a hand to his ear. "Listen."

She grinned. "Listen to what?"

"The contented sounds emanating from that direction. It appears that no one is loudly complaining of starving to death."

She conceded and with a laugh, allowed him to guide her out through the doors that led onto the stone terrace overlooking the park.

"We have it to ourselves," Peyton said. "Arranged perfectly with orchestra taking a break and the guests in at supper."

She shook her head. "And you are taking credit for that?"

"But of course. Timing is everything."

"Ho! You are very good at turning an incident to your advantage, Peyton."

"My sweet," he said softly, "you have no idea."

Her face grew hot, and her belly tightened under his passionate gaze. She loved to banter with him. She'd like to do it for the rest of her life. The soft evening breeze stirred the curls at her temple. What was she thinking? She pushed her hair back into place, the raised arch of scar a bitter reminder. Her chest tightened, and she felt slightly ill. The moment when she must tell him the truth was upon her. Then the enjoyment of the evening would be at an end. So soon. She wanted more time. More…of him.

"Peyton, I—"

"Jason, please."

Nervous, she glanced around, determined not to involve him in gossip. "I can't call you that!"

"Just for tonight?" He took her hands and drew her to the shadowy end of the terrace away from the flaming torches. "Now. No one shall hear but us."

"Jason," she murmured, knowing he would kiss her and helpless to resist.

He gently smoothed a thumb along her bottom lip. "I

like how intimate my name sounds on your lips," he murmured. He lowered his head and covered her mouth with his. An explosion of desire inflamed her, her hands on his nape pulling him closer. Jason gasped and enfolded her snug in his arms. Breathing him in, she melted into him, and her fingers threaded through his silky hair. Held close against his hard chest she never wanted to leave his arms.

Finally, logic won out over the urgent demands of her body. She broke away and placed a hand on his waistcoat to put some space between them. She could feel his heart beating as fast as hers and grew afraid she would cry. "Please. I cannot…"

"Is it because you don't want me?" he asked, his voice low and urgent. "Your kisses prove otherwise."

"No! You must not think that. But I must explain…"

"Is it because of that rakehell, Lawley?"

Horrified, she stared at him. "You know?"

"Lizzie only just told me. She was there that night. I wish I could have dealt with him, sweetheart."

Helen released a long sigh. "I feared you would want to. But I won't allow you to involve yourself in this."

"Is it the only reason you won't marry me?"

She refused to answer, knowing he would discount her fears. She wanted desperately to throw caution to the winds. But she could not, would not, endanger him and tried to explain. "When I heard that shot in the library and feared it was you who had been hurt, it almost brought me to my knees. Even if you gave me your promise not to approach him, Lawley is the revengeful sort. He would challenge you.

I don't believe you would refuse that challenge. Now that his father has died and he's inherited a baronetcy, I am certain he will return soon to claim it."

She held a finger to his lips when he tried to interrupt her. "There's something I've never told anyone, not even my mother. After that night when he...Lawley bailed me up in Bond Street when I was shopping with my maid, just before he left England. He furiously stood over me and would have struck me if the street hadn't been so busy. He blamed me for his father disowning him and threatened to find me when he returned to England and." — she swallowed the lump blocking her throat and dropped her head with the shame of it — "have me again."

"The devil!" Jason growled. "I only wish I could call him out." He cupped her chin, raising her eyes to his. "Darling, Helen. You have such little faith in me. I just delivered a pair of slippery customers to Bow Street tonight before they escaped justice. I am perfectly capable of dealing with someone like Lawley. But..."

"You cannot—."

He shook his head when she would argue. "Listen, my love. Lawley will never return. I've made inquiries about him at Horse Guards. He's dead."

"Dead?" She clutched his arm when her knees threatened to give way. "When? How?"

"Quite recently. The news has only just reached London. Knifed in some Calais tavern. He was on his way home to England."

Helen struggled to believe it. She knew the hateful man's threat had been real and had expected him at every ball and soirée she'd attended since. Then all the humiliation and distress and fear would have returned with him. Now, he never would. She blinked back the rush of tears.

"Cry if you must, my love. You have been so brave." Jason drew a cambric square from his pocket and gently dried the tears on her cheeks.

With a tremulous smile, she clutched his lapel and sniffed. Her body seemed to have lost its ability to remain upright without assistance. "You can't know what hearing this means to me."

"I can only guess at it, sweetheart." He pocketed his handkerchief. "So, now if you can offer no further reason to refuse me?" He sank gracefully down on one knee. "Will you marry me, Helen?"

"Oh yes, yes." She pulled at his hands. "Get up, please. Your clothes will be quite ruined."

"My valet will forgive me when he hears the reason. Bit of a romantic is Hicks."

When he rose, she studied his dear face. "Are you sure, Peyton?"

"Jason," he amended. "I want you very much, Helen. But are *you* sure, sweetheart?"

With a nod, she looped her arms around his neck.

Jason wasted no time in kissing her.

"Father will be pleased," she said when their kiss ended and she began to think clearly again.

"I hope he will."

"You don't know how much. Jason was an ancient Greek hero. *The Argonauts*. Think how well you will fit into the family."

He threw back his head and laughed. "Does that mean that our children will all be called after ancient Greeks?"

"I'm afraid it will be expected. I don't care for some of them either." She grinned. "It has become a family tradition, which I felt you should be warned about. You don't want to change your mind?"

"No, but I draw the line at Aeson or Iolcos," he said huskily. He kissed her lingeringly again.

Her pulse raced. She still couldn't believe it. Was Lawley really dead? "Why do you want to marry me?"

"Why?" He paused. "Apart from the fact that my breath catches in my throat every time I see you?"

She breathed deeply, trying not to cry. He had that same effect on her.

"The first time I met you, I was struck with how unselfishly you cared for others. It's time someone took care of you, my love. And made things right. I want to give you the kind of life you were meant to live. I can't claim it's entirely unselfish of me. I hope you will lavish some of that love and affection you have for your family on me."

"I want to, Jason," she choked on the words. "Very much. I love you so. I think I always did."

His mouth curved with tenderness. "No, my love. Not at first. You were distrustful and suspicious of me."

"Well, yes, that's true. But even so, I wanted you."

Jason's green eyes, raw with need, locked with hers. "Just how much *do* you want me?"

"This much." She kissed him with a passion she never believed herself capable of.

"Peyton?" A young voice came from the door.

They broke apart as Toby shuffled forward, yawning

behind his hand. He eyed Helen with surprise, which faded as he addressed Jason. "You promised to introduce me to Mr. Nash, Peyton. He's here tonight, you know."

~~~

In the ballroom, Jason cast a possessive glance at Helen, slender and seemingly fragile in her lilac gown. He knew that to be deceiving. She was brave, capable, and strong. She'd spoken very fondly of Cherrywood and her dog, Bertie. He hoped she would come to love Peyton Grove.

At the news, Lady Kinsey, elegant in a gold turban and flowing bronze silk, cried and begged a handkerchief from her husband.

Lord Kinsey shook Jason's hand. "Congratulations, Peyton. I knew immediately that you were the man for Helen. I'm delighted you were able to convince her of it." He kissed Helen on both cheeks. "I see I shall have to manage without you on my travels, my dear."

Jason could detect little disappointment behind Kinsey's words and suspected he hadn't wanted the distraction of a vulnerable young woman while he delved into the mysteries of the East.

"I would prefer us to marry soon." Jason smiled at his fiancée. "But Helen feels we should wait until the Season ends, don't you, my love? To offer our support to Diana."

"That might be prudent. A hasty marriage causes gossip," Lady Kinsey said. "And heaven knows we've suffered enough of that."

"And will no doubt suffer more of it," Kinsey said. "Our

children tend to thumb their noses at etiquette." They followed his gaze to where Diana stood laughing with several young men grouped around her. "Let the gossipers say what they like. Time takes care of that nonsense. I can see how well Diana handles the young beaux. She is a force to be reckoned with. And Helen has spent her whole life supporting others. It is time she considered her own needs."

Kinsey's jovial expression slid into a wry grin. "But I advise you to lend a word of advice to your brother. That's a match I won't condone. He's still wet behind the ears."

Jason laughed. "Charlie is about to return to Oxford. In a year, he will take the grand tour. It will be several years before he is able to court Diana."

"Mm. But the Peytons seem a determined lot," Kinsey said. "I expect your brother will turn up again, although I'm not sure Diana will be waiting. Several other gentlemen here tonight have a similar idea."

"I'm sure they do," Jason agreed. "But Charlie is the only young beau Lady Diana has favored with two dances."

Kinsey chuckled. "I believe you are right. But come, we'll announce the engagement before the next dance is called."

After a fanfare from the orchestra, Jason joined Helen and her parents on the dais. Kinsey, at his most effusive, addressed the guests. "My wife and I are thrilled to announce the engagement of our beloved eldest daughter, Lady Helen, to Jason, Captain Lord Peyton. A better fellow for my daughter I could not have found should I have searched the kingdom."

"I thought you were searching the kingdom, and a good deal more besides, Kinsey," called Lord Liverpool. It was followed by good-natured laughter.

As they stepped off the dais to tumultuous applause, Charlie came to slap Jason on the back. "I approve, Jas. Helen is lovely. You're marrying into a splendid family."

Jason watched as his brother smiled at Diana and she smiled back, revealing those fetching dimples. Charlie was returning to Oxford not a moment too soon.

Lizzie kissed them both. "I've always wanted a sister, and now I have two."

"I hope you will come to stay with us at Peyton Grove after the wedding," Helen said. "Our door will always be open."

Lizzie turned to him. "Don't worry Jas, I shall leave you two alone for a decent period."

"After our honeymoon trip, Lizzie." He suspected Peyton Grove would be constantly filled with those seeking respite and some mothering from Helen. Was it unreasonable of him to want to have her to himself?

"What trip?" Helen asked, surprised. "You haven't mentioned it."

"Haven't I? I believe a waltz has been announced, Lady Helen."

Her eyes sparkled. "I believe it has, Lord Peyton."

He led her to the dance floor and swept her into his arms.

"Are you going to tell me?"

"You'll need light muslin dresses and broad-brimmed hats."

"Somewhere hot?" Her eyes sparkled. "It can't be

England."

"I'll arrange a trip to Egypt, for a few weeks after our wedding. I'd like us to spend some time at Peyton Grove first."

She laughed up at him. "Jason! I believed my seeing Egypt was as likely as going to the moon."

He smiled at her. "I would give you the moon if I could, sweetheart."

CHAPTER NINETEEN

Diana yawned as she plaited her hair before the mirror. "Did you see some of the debutantes' faces when your engagement was announced?"

Helen looked up from tying the ribbons on her nightgown. "No." She had seen only Jason.

"They and their mothers looked fit to burst," Diana said gleefully. "Many had hopes in Peyton's direction."

"It's ever such exciting news, Lady Helen," Mary said as she put away their dresses. "I'm so happy for you."

"Thank you, Mary. You must sleep late tomorrow. I don't expect to see you until luncheon."

Mary grinned, bobbed, and left the room.

"I didn't know Peyton had a younger brother," Diana said when she and Helen climbed into bed.

Helen blew out the candle. Breathing in the light scent of smoke, she lay down. "Yes. He's very likeable."

"He is even more gorgeous than Peyton. And much younger. Peyton is almost middle-aged."

Helen grinned into the dark. "And therefore, perfect for

a spinster of advanced years like me."

"I am so happy for you, dearest," Diana said for the umpteenth time. "I knew Peyton would not take no for an answer."

"I am very pleased he didn't," Helen murmured with a rush of feeling. "But enough about me. I do hope your ball was everything you hoped for."

"Everything and more." Diana fell back against the pillows with a sigh. "I met so many nice gentlemen."

"I expect the calling cards will arrive in vast numbers in a few hours," Helen said. "And it is almost dawn. We should get some sleep."

"I'm too excited to sleep."

"Me too. No gentleman caught your attention? What about the marquess' son?"

"He has lovely manners."

"Oh? That doesn't sound like a ringing endorsement. I imagine you will get to know him better during the Season."

Diana propped her head on her hand. "I'm not interested in choosing anyone yet."

"Why not? I'm sure one or two would make perfectly respectable husbands."

"Some would," Diana agreed. "But I intend to enjoy several Seasons of flirting and dancing before I marry."

"Then I'm relieved not to have to chaperone you." Helen turned on the pillow to face her sister. "While I agree it's sensible to take your time, why wait years? You are always saying how love is everything."

"And so, it is. I plan to fall desperately in love, dearest. Just like you." Diana yawned and prodded her pillow. "But I can wait."

"Wait for whom?" Suspicious, Helen poked her sister in the arm. "Did Peyton's brother ask you to wait for him?"

Diana giggled. "Not in so many words."

"Good, because he has no right—"

"But Charlie was quite the most handsome man there. And the only one who made me laugh."

"It's Charlie, is it?" Helen groaned. "Mama says that men who can woo a woman with humor are definitely dangerous. She is referring to Papa, of course." She laughed, thinking of how often their parents joked with one another.

Diana settled onto her side. "I can't wait to hear about your plans. Your wedding, the ring, Peyton's country estate…" Her voice drifted off.

After several moments of silence, Helen bent over her. Diana was asleep.

She lay back and hugged her arms around herself and thought of Jason, his handsome face, his kisses, his humor, his kindness. Realizing that he would soon be her husband made her curl her toes. The thought of such intimacy took her breath away. He was meeting Papa tomorrow to discuss the marriage settlement. The wedding would take place at Walcott, and Mama was already making lists.

~~~

The next day, Jason made his way to Bow Street. He found Bianchi and his accomplice, Barrett, sharing a reeking cell with a man deep in his cups who was singing off key.

The Italian ran to clutch the bars as Jason approached. Bianchi's right eye was swollen shut and his lip cut. "I shall have you arrested for assault," he snarled. "I'm waiting for my solicitor to arrive. Then we shall see who is in the wrong. You have nothing on me. I demand my property returned. Where are my valuable artworks? They could be stolen by now."

"A Mr. Smith, an expert on art forgery, is at present evaluating them. I believe you sold the *Titian* to Lady Braidwood? She has engaged her lawyers, who are most interested in the outcome, as is Gillies and several other members of the *ton*. I must allow that the paintings are skillfully done. I gather it's your work, Barrett? If that is your real name?" A glimmer of pride brightened Barrett's eyes before he sat down with his head in his hands.

Bianchi scowled, winced, and put a hand gingerly to his lip.

"And what might we call you?" Jason persisted. "It can't be Bianchi. He remains in Florence, residing in the villa that you described in such loving detail." He stared into the imposter's furious face. For once the loquacious man made no response.

"I'm afraid you will remain here until you come up before the magistrate," Jason said with great satisfaction. "Regrettably, the accommodation and the food might not meet with your standards."

Jason rode home on horseback, after exercising his chestnut gelding, Icarus, in the park for an hour. He enjoyed being outdoors, although it failed to live up to the fresh country air. He, Charlie, and Lizzie were to have dinner with the Kinseys that evening. Before then, he would need a stern word with Charlie. He and Helen would be the only ones flirting tonight.

As he entered the stable yard and dismounted, his thoughts returned to his sister. Lizzie was a more delicate matter. Would she slip back into the doldrums again? He could not allow it and must try to draw her out. He threw the reins to the stable boy and strode to the house. He would ask Helen to help him.

Jason soon realized his wish for a speedy wedding would have proved difficult for Lady Kinsey to organize. The date was set for six weeks hence, after Kinsey's brother, Lord Nicholas' wedding took place. Jason knew how to employ the time. He would squire Helen around Town during the Season. She deserved to be courted, and he wanted her to enjoy all that she had missed over the years. When their betrothal had been announced at the ball, the expressions on a few of the guests' faces were explicit. Would the old gossip be regurgitated? He and Helen would show the *ton* how happy and perfectly suited they were. If that failed to convince some, he would deal with it. And not necessarily politely.

CHAPTER TWENTY

The Kentish sky over Walcott resembled a Gainsborough painting of an English summer, azure blue banked up with puffy, gilt-edged clouds. A light breeze stirred the leaves of the stately trees in the park. Toby appeared in view, gesticulating madly while walking with Mr. Nash over the lawn, two hounds capering ahead.

Helen turned from the window as Diana came into the bedroom she had all to herself. "The weather is going to be perfect."

"I heard a carriage arrive," Diana said.

"I wonder if it's Jason's." Helen went to open the door leading onto the Juliette balcony. She saw a dark-haired man walking up the drive beyond the box hedges and knew instinctively it was Jason. Her heart leaped and she warmed all over.

"Don't go out there in your wrap." Diana laughed. "You cannot see Peyton until the wedding."

She couldn't resist peeking at him, before he disappeared around the corner of the house. Helen drew an excited breath and turned again to admire her wedding dress carefully laid out awaiting her. Cream silk satin overlaid with cream silk net, decorated with satin ribbon and intricate embroidery. She touched the feather-light short veil to be held in place by a circlet of diamonds and pearls. A gown from her dreams.

The preceding two months had been a whirlwind of balls, routs, dinners, and dances at Almack's. Despite being squired by one of the most handsome men in the *ton*, or perhaps because of it, she was subjected to the odd nasty comment in the ladies withdrawing room. She kept it to herself, knowing Mama would be upset and Jason might get angry. In time, that chapter of her life would fade into the past. Already a royal scandal had erupted to fill the gossip sheets and distract any attention from her.

Mama entered the room. "Diana, can you make sure Alexander isn't spreading his breakfast over his coat? Mrs. Prince has other duties, and he insisted on putting on his velvet suit."

Diana laughed. "Zander considers that his role, carrying the ring on a velvet cushion, is the most important part of the wedding."

Earlier, Zander had assured Helen that he was big now and would be perfectly all right without her. "Diana has promised to read to me every night," he'd said, looking anxious. Helen would make sure that if Diana or her mother couldn't then someone else would.

After Diana left, Mama sat on the blue silk damask sofa, which matched the curtains and the bed hangings in the elegant room. The silk wallpaper patterned with lotus flowers and birds was the blue color of a Ming vase.

Mama patted the cushion beside her. Helen obeyed, ready for one of their talks, although this time she welcomed it.

"Were you able to sleep, my dear? I confess I didn't the night before my wedding. I remember your grandmother fussing over my puffy eyes. She cooled a spoon with ice water and applied the back of it to my lower lids, which did the trick perfectly. You won't require it. You look radiant."

"I did manage a few hours."

"It's been a busy couple of months, hasn't it? And you and Peyton have not been able to spend much time alone."

Helen gave her mother a wry smile. "We talked a lot." And she'd learned more about his past, his relationship with his father and how the war affected him, although he hadn't put it into words. She came to realize how much he cared for his brother and sister. Lizzie had attended every venue with them. Helen enjoyed her company while Diana was occupied, always with at least one or two admirers hanging on her every word.

In a quiet moment, when Jason was absent, Lizzie had confessed that she hadn't met anyone she'd warmed to. "The older gentlemen are generally very reserved. If I marry again, I want to laugh with someone. I want passion."

Helen could only agree with her but reassured her that there was someone who would suit her perfectly. She had only to wait for him.

"I thought the strict chaperoning appropriate," Mama said, bringing Helen back to the present. "In the circumstances."

She understood that her mother did not want to give

any of the gossips fuel to use against her. But it had been difficult. While Jason had readily agreed and was scrupulous about protecting her reputation, he still managed to find moments to pull her behind pillars and potted plants and into empty corridors. Each hurried kiss held a promise of their wedding night. She was a little nervous, but yearned for it as much as he did.

She took a deep breath. Tonight, they would finally be alone together.

While her parents had decided on this big, grand wedding, Helen would have preferred a smaller more intimate one. The house was already abuzz with early guests filling the reception rooms while their servants were taken down to the servants' hall.

After a private ceremony in the chapel, the wedding breakfast would follow. Two hundred guests would fill the enormous ballroom, where tables had been set up around the dance floor. A full orchestra was hired. The preparations all seemed to happen like magic. Helen had nothing to do but cosset herself. Walcott ran like a well-oiled machine.

Speeches would be made, and even Harry had abandoned what he'd called the fleshpots of Paris to come home to deliver one. It made her even more nervous. There were many wonderful childhood memories to draw from, as well as some embarrassing ones. She only hoped her brother would choose wisely. She expected he would. His shoulders broader, he seemed to have grown taller and more mature.

A footman knocked at the bedroom door and brought in a fragrant tray containing a pot of chocolate, cups and saucers, and sweet rolls. He bowed and left them. Grandfather's staff never put a foot wrong. Until the antics made him chuckle, she'd always considered the butler, Gibson, terribly snooty. Helen drew in a deep breath. She had yet to see her new home and tackle the staff.

Helen's hand shook slightly as she poured out the chocolate.

"Are you nervous, dear?" Mama asked.

"A little. It's such a big wedding."

"Your father and I thought it best."

She leaned against her mother, drinking her warming cup of chocolate, savoring the sweet taste. "I know why you decided that. You always know the right thing to do. I am so very grateful to you and Papa. I feared I am a disappointment to you."

"Never, my sweet girl." Mama hugged her. "You deserve the best, Helen. And God willing, you have found it in a good man.

"Now, your first night with Peyton," she said briskly, putting down her cup. "I believe it's always good for a young woman to have some idea of what to expect. I know you feel you're not an innocent, but darling, believe me, you are. Sit still and listen, and then you may ask questions if you wish."

"Send for Mary, it's time to dress for the ceremony at eleven o'clock." Mama rose, leaving Helen blushing furiously after a talk which proved enlightening, but failed to banish her nerves.

A half hour later, Helen stood before the mirror as Diana arranged her veil. She was very pleased with the result. Her skin looked creamy, and her eyes sparkled.

"You look beautiful, Helen."

"Thank you, dearest." Perhaps love made one beautiful, Helen thought.

Mary handed her the bouquet of white roses and peonies. And, with a deep breath, she descended the staircase with Diana to the hall where their father waited, a hand on the bannister, smiling up at them.

Helen advanced down the aisle on her father's arm in the exquisitely painted chapel, decorated and perfumed with white flowers. Diana followed, in pale blue, with Zander, serious in a gray velvet suit, holding the ring on its pillow. She smiled at Uncle Nicholas who sat next to Harry and winked at her. Her distinguished, elegant grandfather gave her an approving nod.

Mama smiled teary-eyed from the front pew.

Jason waited at the altar with Charlie, his groomsman. Two tall handsome men in dark blue and crisp white with camellia boutonnieres.

Helen looked up into Jason's warm, appreciative gaze. "You are *so* beautiful," he murmured.

The vicar cleared his throat. "Dearly beloved…"

When her father stepped forward to give her away, Helen's eyes blurred with tears. She was leaving his care forever and moving forward into a new life. And though she welcomed it, she couldn't help a pang of loss.

The vicar cleared his throat, and the ceremony began.

Zander had managed, walking slowly with great care, to hand over the ring. His duty done, he smiled his singularly sweet smile and scurried back to Mama.

Her glove removed, Jason took her hand in his.

"With this ring, I thee wed..."

His gaze rested on her as he repeated: "With my body I thee worship..."

Then the vicar spoke the final words, "I pronounce that they be man and wife..."

Man and wife! Helen kissed her husband and smiled into his ardent green eyes.

After the signing of the register, all was a blur. A wonderful rejoicing, thanking hundreds of guests for their blessings, picking at the rich, exotic foods while her mother urged her to eat. And trying not to drink too much champagne. The deep pride she felt when her father spoke in glowing terms of his eldest daughter. Then laughing with Jason as Harry, his bright blue eyes alight with mischief, described her failure to accomplish fly fishing, despite his supreme patience, and her auspicious beginnings as an equestrian, when the bad-tempered pony she had as a child threw her into a hedge. He ended with how she could add up sums when they played cards, faster than anyone he knew and, surprisingly, beat him once or twice at chess.

Then the orchestra struck up, and Jason swept her expertly over the floor for the bridal waltz before everyone joined in.

Now she stood once again in her bedroom, slightly dizzy, a married lady. Mary helped her dress as she became aware that she would soon say goodbye to everything she had known up until this moment. In the mirror, she was pleased with how smart she looked in her new celestial blue pelisse, the hat of spotted blue velvet adorned with a plume of ostrich feathers, her half-boots of lemon kid leather. A surge of excitement spun through her as she arranged her India shawl over her shoulders.

The weather, which had been perfect all day, threatened rain. It would be some hours before she and Jason could be alone. He had invited Mary to travel with them rather than wait for his valet, who was to follow along later.

Helen leaned out of the carriage window and waved a final goodbye to her family, dwarfed by Walcott's six towering pillars as they gathered on the mosaic-tiled portico. Inside, the ballroom was still full of guests, some of whom would stay for several days.

She sat back against the well-padded leather squabs while Jason held her hand, his warm gaze resting on her. Was he as she was, thinking of their wedding night?

The carriage pulled away and rattled along the avenue of ancient gnarled trees. They had begun their four-hour journey to Surrey and Peyton Grove.

EPILOGUE

The weather had turned the roads to mud and made the traveling difficult and slow. Dusk had fallen before the carriage passed through the tall, wrought-iron gates of Peyton Grove.

"We're here?" Helen left the comfort of his arm to peer through the window.

"Pity your first glimpse of my home isn't in daylight," Jason said, "but you will see it tomorrow."

"I shall get up very early."

"I think not," Jason said with a laugh in his voice.

Helen was glad of the poor light, sure her face was crimson. Fortunately, Mary was intent on gathering together the things she had brought with her.

The carriage lamps cast a small glow as the vehicle trundled along the drive through what appeared to be a large park.

"After this next turn, we shall see the house," Jason said.

"I can't wait," she breathed. Even Mary pressed her nose to the window.

The warm summer air was drenched with sweet perfumes from the garden. The house came into view on a slight rise. Smaller than Walcott and newer than Cherrywood, the cream stone walls of the three-story dwelling were covered in a white flowering creeper, the long windows alight with candles. Golden light spilled from the open front doors onto the columned portico.

The tall, thin butler stepped forward. "Good evening, my lord."

"Helen, meet Russell, my indispensable butler. He and a few of the staff have come from London to serve us."

"Welcome, my lady."

"Thank you, Russell." Helen liked the look of the man who had a kind face. The first hurdle over, she asked if Mary could be introduced to the staff and then directed upstairs to her bedroom.

Russell bowed. "Certainly, Lady Peyton."

"We shall dine in an hour, Russell. Please advise Cook."

Jason took her hand and led her through the house. Drawing her along, her arm tucked in his, they walked from the gallery through the elegant blue drawing room and morning rooms to the dining room. He showed her, with some pride, his study, and the library, and they returned to climb the stairs to the bedrooms.

Jason opened the door to the master suite decorated in gold and royal blue and then led her through a sitting room to her own bedroom, charmingly decorated in lilac and yellow floral wallpaper. He gathered her into his arms.

His gaze was a soft caress. "Do you approve?"

"Of your beautiful home, yes, very much. Of you, very much indeed."

"It's your home, too, my sweet bride."

At Mary's knock on the door, he drew away regretfully. "I'll leave you to change, my love."

~~~

After dinner, they'd strolled in the perfumed, velvety night air until the time came for Helen to wait for him in her bedchamber. While Jason washed and cleaned his teeth, he cautioned himself to tread carefully tonight. He knew how to pleasure a woman and leave her satisfied. But his lovers were always experienced and knew how to take their own pleasure. Although Helen wasn't technically a virgin, she might just as well be. He doubted she would have had more than a glimpse of an erect male, and never a naked one. And his body was already taut and eager to make love to her.

He must summon patience, to make sure she was comfortable and confident, her passions aroused.

Opening the door, he saw her propped up in bed, a welcoming, yet strained smile on her lips. He sat down on the bed in his dressing gown and raised her hand to his lips. "You look lovely with your hair down. That's a pretty nightgown."

She put a hand to her bosom, reminding him that she wore nothing beneath it. "Yes, isn't it? White lawn and lace are always so…"

He undid buttons that hid her from him, planning to purchase her some nightgowns. Something filmier, less opaque. Red perhaps, Helen would look wonderful in red. Parting the ruffles, he leaned forward and kissed the throbbing pulse at the base of her throat. After her bath, her skin was dewy and warm and petal soft. She smelled of roses.

"I want you so much," he murmured.

"Shall we snuff out the candles?"

Jason was not about to let her hide from him. They must deal with her past here and now.

"No, my love," he said gently. He stood and undid the belt on his emerald green and black silk robe. Slipping out of it, he threw it on the bottom of the bed and stood naked before her.

Helen's gaze roamed appreciatively over him. "You are very decorative, Lord Peyton."

He laughed, pleased to find she wasn't coy. He knew she wouldn't be. But neither did she seem too nervous, and that reassured him.

He pulled back the bedcovers. "Shall we remove this?"

She helped him pull the nightgown over her head then lay back naked. She didn't try to cover herself, but her eyes looked anxious as he gazed at her.

"I knew you would be beautiful."

He braced himself on each side of her and leaned down to kiss her. "I'll be gentle, Helen."

"I know."

When he settled half over her, she smiled. "I am so blessed, my darling." Her fingers tangled in his hair then roamed across his back and down, as if exploring every muscle, bone, and sinew.

He cupped her head, and his mouth sought hers, tasting her and breathing in her aroused womanly fragrance with a gasp of pleasure as passion and a desire to join with her raged through him. He explored her full breasts and thumbed the pert brown nipples and, eliciting an excited gasp, lowered his head to suckle on each one.

His hand slipped down to the heated place between her legs as he explored her body. He ravished her with his mouth, nibbling and licking as she moaned and shuddered until she was panting and ready for him.

Then he slipped between her thighs and gently entered her with a loud groan.

~~~

They made love again during the night, and two hours after the sun rose, she wakened and saw him sleeping beside her, one muscled arm thrown over his head. She leaned close and traced a finger across his strong jaw, the beginnings of a dark beard rasping beneath her touch. How exquisite the lovemaking was. She never expected it could be like this. Jason had been gentle and forceful, lithe, and strong. Under his clever hands and mouth, she was all sensation, her body vibrating, enraptured, the joining of their bodies so profound it brought tears to her eyes. Before sleep claimed them, they had talked about all manner of things, from her love of cooking to his penchant for poetry. Finally, she'd fallen asleep, her body melting with pleasurable exhaustion and a peacefulness she hadn't known in years.

He opened his green eyes and caught her hand, raising it to his lips. "How are you this morning, sweetheart?"

"I shall be fine after you kiss me."

"Happy to oblige." She giggled as he rolled her over and laid half on top of her. Skin to skin, as things grew heated, there was a knock at the door. Jason cursed and reached for his robe.

Mary entered with a tray of hot chocolate for Helen and coffee for him.

"Please tell your maid not to come until we ring for her," he said grumpily after she'd left.

Helen laughed. "Daylight is streaming in through the break in the curtains. I'm eager to see more of my beautiful new home. The park and gardens looked extensive."

"My grandfather planted a thousand trees, cedars, chestnuts, oaks, and pines, as well as some quite rare species. My grandmother created the rose arbor." Jason took her empty cup from her and put it down on the table. As he gathered her up in his arms, a knock was followed by a shrill barking and scratching at the door. He sighed and called for the footman to enter.

A small terrier ran across the carpet and leaped into Helen's arms. "Bertie!" She cuddled the excited dog. "Oh, Jason. That was so thoughtful of you. I always worry that he might be pining for me. I can't thank you enough."

Jason took the excited dog and dropped him gently to the floor. "I know of an excellent way to thank me."

ABOUT THE AUTHOR

Maggi lives with her husband a retired lawyer, in a quaint old town in the Southern Highlands of New South Wales, Australia. She has a BA in English and an MA in Creative Writing. When not creating stories, she reads, enjoys her garden, long walks and feeding the local wildlife. Her kookaburras (Australian Kingfishers) prefer to be hand fed.

Maggi's books and novellas are Amazon bestsellers in Regency, historical romance, and suspense. She has published more than 25 novels and novellas and writes in several genres, contemporary and historical romance, romantic suspense, and young adult novels.

Maggi draws her inspiration from the novels of Jane Austen, Georgette Heyer and Victoria Holt.

If you enjoyed Unmasking Lady Helen, The Kinsey Family, Book One, an honest review is always appreciated.

Maggi loves to hear from readers. You can contact her through her website.

Like to learn about new releases and freebies? Join her newsletter at: http://www.maggiandersenauthor.com

Where to find Maggi:

Amazon Author Page: https://www.amazon.com/Maggi-Andersen/e/B003MJXQVG/

Blog: http://www.maggiandersen.blogspot.com

Facebook: https://www.facebook.com/maggiandersenauthor/

Twitter:

https://twitter.com/maggiandersen

Goodreads:

https://www.goodreads.com/author/show/2786221.Maggi_Andersen

Pinterest: http://www.pinterest.com/maggiandersen.com

AUTHOR'S BACKLIST

Once a Wallflower Series
Presenting Miss Letitia

Dangerous Lords Series
The Baron's Betrothal
Seducing the Earl
The Viscount's Widowed Lady
Governess to the Duke's Heir

The Baxendale Sisters Regency Series
Lady Honor's Debt
Lady Faith Takes a Leap
Lady Hope and the Duke of Darkness
The Seduction of Lady Charity
The Scandalous Lady Mercy

Regency Sons
Captain Jack Ryder – The Duke's Bastard

The Kinsey Family
Unmasking Lady Helen

Standalone Historical Romances
Seduced by the Pirate – Pirates of Britannia
The Marquess Meets His Match
Hostage to Love
A Gift From A Goddess – A Legend To Love
How to Tame a Rake
An Improper Earl
Caroline and the Captain
The Earl and the Highwayman's Daughter

Stirring Passions
At the Earl's Convenience
Lord Bartholomew's Christmas Bride
The Duke's Mysterious Lady
What A Gentleman Desires
Diary of a Painted Lady
On Scandalous Night
The Mystery at Falconbridge Hall

Contemporary Romantic Suspense
Murder in Devon
With Murderous Intent
Twined
Finding Daniel

Box Sets
Dangerous Lords
The Baxendale Sisters

Young Adult
Waving at the Moon

Non-Fiction

Castle's Customs, and Kings: True Tales by English Historical
Fiction Authors

www.ingramcontent.com/pod-product-compliance
Lightning Source LLC
Chambersburg PA
CBHW031317170626
46807CB00002B/454